THE SCORE

A SINGLE IN SEATTLE NOVEL

KRISTEN PROBY

&
AMPERSAND
PUBLISHING, INC.

The Score

A Single in Seattle Novel

By

Kristen Proby

THE SCORE

A Single in Seattle Novel

Kristen Proby

Cover Design: Emily Wittig Designs

For every girl who ever thought they weren't enough.
You're everything.

PROLOGUE

SOPHIE

Fifteen Years Ago

She's dead.
        I just can't believe it. I mean, I was at the funeral, and everyone was so sad, and Steph hasn't been at school. She doesn't return my calls or texts.

She's gone.

But how can that be?

I pull out the notebook we passed back and forth during lunch from under my pillow and stare at it. In her handwriting on the cover, it says, *Fitness Journal.*

We were just trying to be thin.

To be accountable, we'd pass this notebook between us and write down what we ate, how much of it, and how long we waited until we threw it back up again.

I don't blow chunks easily, so it was hard, but it had just started to work. I could see a difference in how my clothes fit.

And then she died.

For the first time since I found out about her death, I feel tears gather. Did we do something wrong?

My God, I don't want to die.

And I don't like keeping secrets from my parents.

My little brother, Liam, is already in bed, so I take the notebook downstairs where my parents are curled up on the couch, watching some sci-fi show.

"Mom?"

They turn and look at me, and when they see me crying, Dad immediately turns off the TV, and I move to sit in the chair across from them.

"What's wrong?" Mom asks as she and Dad lean forward. "Are you hurt?"

"I don't know." I wipe away a tear. "She's really dead, isn't she?"

"Oh, baby." Mama reaches for my hand. "Yes. She is."

"How?"

"They're still running the autopsy," Dad says softly. "They aren't entirely sure why she passed away in her sleep, honey."

"I might know. I think it might be because of this." I swallow hard and then pass them the notebook, and it all just comes flooding out of me. "I told her that I wanted to be skinnier. You always say that I'm perfect just the way I am, but I'm fat."

"You are *not* fat," Dad insists. "You're thirteen, and your body is changing. A lot of kids go through a phase where they gain weight easily because of hormones, but trust me, it will even out."

"Yeah, well, kids are mean, and they remind me every day that I've gotten fat."

"Kids suck," Mom mutters as she opens the notebook. When she scowls, I know it's not good. "Wait, you were *throwing up* together?"

"*What?*" This comes from Dad.

Yep, not good.

"Steph said she'd been doing it for a long time, and it worked for her. She *was* skinny, and I thought she just knew about it. So, she told me what to do, and I did it. She said it was okay because we let our stomachs absorb some of the food, but then we threw the rest up."

"No." Dad shakes his head and drags his hand down his face. "No, Sophie."

"You don't understand," I counter, but I keep my voice calm. It never works to raise my voice to my father. I learned that a long time ago. "Everyone in our family is beautiful. Do you know what it's like to have all of these celebrities for aunts and uncles but I look like *this?*"

"Okay," Mom says, holding up her hands. "First of

all, I don't know what you *think* you look like, Soph, but you're a beautiful girl. Thirteen is the *worst*, but you won't always be this age. You absolutely can't solve anything by falling into an eating disorder."

"That's not—"

"Honey, this is an eating disorder. It's not a diet plan —no thirteen-year-old should be on a diet plan, by the way. We feed you healthy meals. You have a balanced diet, and you need that food so you can continue to grow. I have to call Steph's mom."

"No."

"Do you think she'll get in trouble?" Dad demands, true anger firing in his voice. "She's *gone*, honey. She can't get into trouble now, and if this gives her parents some answers, well, then we need to tell them."

"I'm sorry." The tears come in earnest now. "I didn't know that it was wrong."

"Why did you keep it a secret?" Mom asks.

She hands me a tissue, and I wipe my eyes before shrugging a shoulder.

"That's what I thought," she continues. "If you thought you had to keep it a secret, then you knew that something about it wasn't right. You *won't* do this anymore."

"No." I shake my head. "I promise, I won't. That won't be me, Mama."

"There will be therapy," Dad says, leaving no room for argument. "And, if we need one, a nutritionist. I won't lose you, Sophie. Not today or any other day."

4

I jump up and rush to him, sit in his lap, and bury my nose in his neck the way I used to when I was younger.

"I'm so sorry," I say again, soaking in the safety of my daddy's arms. "I'm so, so sorry."

CHAPTER 1

SOPHIE

*B*efore I can even ring the bell, the door is thrown open, and Liam, my younger brother, rushes outside.

"Morry," he mutters, his mouth full of something.

"What are you even eating?" I demand as I turn and watch him hurry down the walk to his car.

"Muffin," he says and throws me a smile that all the girls tell me is charming and magnetic.

To me, it just looks like he's about to get into trouble. Which is on-brand for Liam.

"Gotta go. See ya." He waves, drops into his Mustang, and vrooms right out of the driveway and down the street, through the Alki neighborhood of Seattle.

Since the door is open, I walk inside and make a beeline for the kitchen.

Some of the parents of all of us cousins went in on buying this house and then renovated it to suit a bunch of late teens or early twenty-somethings.

My aunt Natalie has owned the house next door for*ever*. And now that the family owns this house, too, the parents decided to take down the fence that separated the two properties and make it a sort of Montgomery cousin compound.

We're just a regular bunch of west-coast Kennedys.

"What are you up to?" Hudson asks as he reaches for a coffee mug and pours himself a cup. His dark-blond hair is a wild mass of bedhead, and his blue eyes smile at me sleepily as he takes his first sip. "Is someone in trouble?"

"Just because one of us oldies shows up to say hi doesn't always mean that someone is in trouble."

"Not *always*," he concedes. "Did you just miss me and couldn't stay away any longer?"

I smirk and reach for my own mug. "Something like that."

The truth is, I sometimes get lonely in my condo. I work from home, so I'm there by myself most of the time, and sometimes, I miss the chaos that is my family, so I swing by the compound to see what's going on.

"How's school going?" I ask him.

"It's almost over, and it can't come soon enough," he says with a sigh, scratching the stubble on his cheek. "But it's good. I like it."

"Being an electrician was an excellent decision," I inform him.

"Yeah, well, most of my friends thought it was stupid that I didn't go to a university." He sips again, then shrugs. "But I *hated* school, Soph. I wouldn't have been good in a classroom, and I grew up in a construction family."

"That you did." I hold my mug out to clink his. Hud's dad, Mark, and my dad own a construction company together. It's in our blood.

"I can make a good living with this."

"Absolutely, you can. I'm really proud of you, twerp."

He grins. "Thanks. And you're not so bad yourself."

I laugh just as Abby walks in, yawning hugely. "Coffee," she mutters. "Must have coffee."

"We drank the last of it," Hudson says and then smirks when Abby's eyes narrow into slits. "But I'll make more."

"Coffee," she repeats.

Yeah, this is just what I needed this morning.

"So, what *are* you up to?" Hudson asks as he fills the pot with water.

"I'm on my way to go for a run, actually, but I thought I'd swing by and see how you guys are doing in the new house."

"The hot water heater stopped working," Abby informs me. She's collapsed on the table, her face buried in her arms. "Cold showers suck ass."

"I fixed it," Hudson reminds her.

"Yeah, but not before I had to take a cold shower." She lifts her head and gazes at him hopefully. "Is it ready yet?"

"No."

She collapses once more.

"The house is pretty epic," Hudson says. "And the cousins' night we're gonna have here this weekend is going to be a blast, especially since we'll be able to go back and forth between both houses."

"The weather has been looking up," I add. "So, we might not have to make the journey in the rain."

"It's spring," Abby reminds us. "And Seattle. At least we're not still stuck under ten feet of snow in Iceland."

"You loved Iceland," I remind my cousin. The entire family, all four thousand of us, descended on Iceland for Christmas. It was fabulous.

"I did, but I don't want to live in *that* kind of snow."

"It's gonna snow?"

And now, I've seen the whole household as Zoey, the youngest of this bunch, joins us.

"No, we were talking about Iceland."

"I think I want to move there," Zoey says with a fanciful sigh and sits at the table next to Abby.

"Your dad would *kill* you," Hudson says with a laugh. "No way Uncle Will wants his baby girl halfway around the world."

"I'm a grown-up," Zoey mumbles with a scowl. "And I need coffee."

"It's almost done," Hudson replies.

"I should go." I stand and set my empty mug in the dishwasher. "I have some filming to do after my run, but I wanted to swing by and say hi."

"I like it when you come by and I'm not in trouble," Hud says before giving me a side hug. "Be safe out there. People suck."

"Same goes."

I wave and close the front door behind me, then hurry down the walkway to my car. Coming over here was two-fold.

To see the cousins and my brother, *and* so that I had a decent place to park while I go for a run on the waterfront.

It's my favorite place to run in the city.

The trail spans over five miles, so I can go as far as I want, and the view can't be beat.

The Seattle skyline is always beautiful, but this morning, it's also clear enough to see Mount Rainier in the distance, and it makes me smile.

I love my home.

With my earbuds in—but not loud enough to drown out my surroundings—I take off down the path, headed away from the city first. I want that view to be my reward on the way back.

I let the rhythm of the music set my cadence. Losing myself in the run is a drug that I never thought I'd become addicted to, but here we are anyway.

And the fact that I'm not stick-thin always garners

looks from passersby, who can't believe that a curvy girl can be fit enough to run.

But I stopped caring about what others think of my body a long time ago. Now, it's my job to help other women stop caring about what others think of their bodies, too.

I turn a corner, getting ready to head back the way I came, when, out of nowhere, a big body slams into me and takes us both down to the ground.

One of my earbuds falls out, stopping the music.

"Oh, God."

I try to roll away, but I'm pinned.

"I don't have any money."

"Shit." The man, the very *heavy* man, raises his head and gives it a shake, as if he's dizzy. "Oh, man. I'm so sorry."

"Get. Off. Can't. Breathe." I push on his very sweaty, very *bare* chest. "Off."

"Oh, right." He rolls away, and I take in a gasping breath. "Shit, I'm sorry."

He holds out a hand to help me to my feet, and I accept. His hand is firm and a little calloused.

"I looked down at my watch for just a second, and then you were suddenly there, and—"

"And you plowed me over." I search the grass for the missing earbud.

"What are we looking for?" He searches with me, which is kind of endearing. *Geez, I think the tackler is endearing? I must be concussed.* "Keys?"

"Earbud."

"Ah." After a few seconds, he reaches down and picks it up. "Found it. You know, you shouldn't listen to music while you run. Especially alone. You need to be aware of your surroundings."

I narrow my eyes on him as I take my earbud out of his hand and ignore his sexy torso. He's *tall.* He must be the same height as my dad and all my uncles, and they're a bunch of tall guys.

It's where I get my height from.

"Thanks for the advice." I slip it back into my ear. "I can hear everything over the music."

"Did I hurt you?"

"Nothing that an Epsom salt bath won't cure. Be careful out there."

And with that, I turn and jog away. When I turn the corner to circle back around, I see that he's still watching me, and when I run past him, I simply say, "Don't be a creep."

"No, ma'am," I hear him mutter, and when my back is to him, I grin.

If I had to get tackled in the park, a sexy tackler was the way to go.

TODAY IS A FILMING DAY, so when I get home, I hop in the shower and get myself ready. I'm known for not wearing a ton of makeup, but I do put a little on my eyes before pulling my hair back into the ponytail that's also part of my brand. Then, I pick out a pair of teal leggings, a white T-shirt, and a matching teal jacket to go over it before heading to the kitchen.

I always keep most of my recording equipment set up. I'm the only one who lives here, and it's a pain in the ass to take all the lighting gear up and down.

So, it just stays.

Just when I'm about to open the fridge, my assistant, Becs, hurries through the front door.

"I'm late," she says, flailing her arms around. "And I'm sorry."

I glance at the time. "You're literally *one* minute late. We don't start the flogging around here until you're four minutes late. It's in the rules."

She smirks. "Yeah, well, it wasn't easy leaving my warm bed this morning."

"And who was making it so warm?"

Becs licks her lips. "His name is Lenny. He's a *musician.* I mean, he's no Leo Nash or anything, but he plays the harmonica."

I blink at her. "The *harmonica?*"

"Yes, and I didn't realize just how sexy that is until last night."

"Huh. I guess I never considered the harmonica to be a sexy instrument. But whatever floats your boat, Becs."

"Oh, he floated my boat all right."

I wrinkle my nose. "Okay. Enough of that."

"You could use some boat floating of your own, you know."

"My boat is just fine moored in the harbor."

"So *boring.*"

"Maybe, and I know this is a *wild* idea here, but just maybe we could think about work today. We have four videos to shoot, so you'll have to forgive me if I don't want to go into great detail about the lack of boat floating in my life."

"Okay, let's do this. I got all the groceries on your list and put them in the fridge and pantry yesterday."

"I saw that, thanks."

Becs has been with me for three years. She helps me monitor all the social media platforms, and keeps me organized. And twice a week, when we film, she comes to help.

"You got another email from Healthy Food, Inc. this morning."

"The answer is still no."

I set out a cutting board, a knife, and a bowl, and when Becs doesn't say anything at all, I turn to her.

"You might want to at least hear what they have to say. It could be a *lot* of money."

"And they'd have control over my content. They'd tell me what I can and cannot say. This is my *brand*, Becs. I can't sell that off."

"Okay." She nods, but I can see that she doesn't agree.

But this is *my* business, and I do very well with it.

Better than very well.

I just finished writing a book for a major publisher, and they paid me a handsome advance for it. My income from social media streams is in the high six figures.

If anyone is going to take my message globally, it's going to be *me*.

"I want to film the healthy and delicious charcuterie board today, along with the roasted pepper soup, and then we're going to do a short video in my living room, and one where I go over skin care in the bathroom."

"I live for recipe day," Becs says with a happy sigh. "Does this mean I can take home some soup?"

"Of course."

She does a quick happy dance, and then we get down to work.

A NICE CHARCUTERIE spread is one of my uncle Will's favorite things, so I'm taking the one I made on camera today to his and my aunt Meg's house. Of course, Will eats anything and everything he can get his greedy hands on, so I often take a lot of my "extras" over to him.

It's a beautiful spring afternoon in Seattle. But because it's also a Friday, traffic is a nightmare, so it seemingly takes me forever to get through the city, headed to where I need to go.

I frown when I see some cars I don't recognize in the driveway.

I don't want to interrupt anything, so I quickly call Meg.

"Hey, pretty girl. What are you doing?" She always answers the phone in the same way, and it always makes me smile.

"Well, I'm in your driveway, but it looks like I might be interrupting something. I should have called first."

"Nonsense. You know you're always welcome here. Come on in. Will just invited a few of the guys from the team over for a little barbecue."

"Oh, I can come back another—"

"If you don't come in here and save me from all of this testosterone, I will never forgive you."

I laugh, immediately feeling better. "Okay. On my way."

It only takes me a few minutes to gather all of my supplies, and when I open the front door, Meg is hurrying to help me.

"What did you bring?"

"Charcuterie," I reply, letting her take one of the bags from me. "I made it for a video today, and I will never eat it all myself. Uncle Will never turns down food."

"Let's be honest, I don't either. You always make the *best* stuff. Come on in. Will's out back with the guys, enjoying the sunshine while we have it. And I was actually in the kitchen, cleaning out my fridge."

"Oh, good timing. I'll help."

"No, you won't. But you *will* chat with me while I do this. Do you mind if I nibble on what you brought?"

"Of course not. I brought it for you."

Meg and Will's house is something to write home about. It's huge and has a view of the water. As a retired quarterback for the Seattle football team, and maybe one of the most beloved players ever to play the sport, Will did *very* well for himself. He continues to do so as a sports commentator, and he is still active with the team as a mentor.

I don't think wild horses could keep him away. Football runs through his veins.

And Meg is a nurse in the pediatric oncology ward at Seattle Children's.

I love them both so much.

"You clean. I'll put this together," I offer, and begin assembling what's in the bags. "I even brought over a board."

"It's gorgeous. I might keep it."

"It's all yours." I grin and carefully arrange the cheeses, fruits, and veggies. "How are things going now that both Erin and Zoey are living at the compound and you're empty nesters?"

Meg pauses and turns to me with a sigh. "It's been…weird. For more than twenty years, I've had kids to take care of. Meals to cook, laundry, carpooling, all of the things, and now they're gone, and I don't know what to do with some of the time. Hence, a party with the players for Will and fridge cleaning for me."

"I think almost all the parents are feeling the same way. Only Matt and Nic and Dom and Alecia still have a kid at home. Everyone else is grown and doing their thing."

"It freaks me out," she says quietly. "I'm glad that everyone is still here locally. That makes us all feel better."

"But how long can it last?"

Her eyes find mine. "Exactly. Gone are the days of little ones running about at family gatherings. Now we have new worries."

"And maybe grandkids sooner or later. With Liv and Stella both getting married soon, and Josie newly married, it's bound to happen."

Meg's eyes fill with tears. "Oh, you're right."

"Okay, don't cry. I didn't come over for that."

"Grandkids." She sniffles, then shakes her head. "Time just flies by."

"You sound like my mom. Here, cry into this gouda."

Meg laughs and reaches for the snack. "Cheese makes everything better."

"Hell yes, it does."

"Did you hear that Liv and Vaughn set their date?" she asks me as she chews. "This is really good, by the way."

"Right? No, I hadn't heard yet. When?"

19

"Next month."

I blink at her. "What? Next *month?*"

"Yes, and they're not telling anyone except close family and friends because they don't want a media circus. Liv wants it out at the vineyard where we can control security better, and it's just so pretty out there anyway that it's perfect."

"*Your* wedding was there," I say with a smile. "I think it's perfect, too. And fast."

"I think, when you're as high profile as Vaughn is, you have to make it fast. Otherwise, things leak, and the press can ruin *everything.*"

"We know all about that." I pop an olive into my mouth. "Well, that's exciting. I bet she makes her dress herself. I'll have to call her."

"I think all of us girls should get together to drink cocktails and talk about all the details," Meg says. "In fact, I'll invite everyone over here next weekend."

"I'm in." We cheers with our crackers, just as Uncle Will walks into the room.

"I didn't know you were here."

He scoops me up into a big hug.

"I brought food."

"My favorite."

"Every food is your favorite." He grins in that cocky way he does that always makes me laugh. "I hear you're having a party."

"That's right. Oh, I want to introduce you to someone."

He steps back, and I see that someone followed Will into the room.

And when I see who it is, I feel my eyes go wide.

It's *him*.

The guy who tackled me this morning.

"We've met," he says.

CHAPTER 2

IKE

*I*t's as though I conjured her out of my mind. Manifested her into standing before me. I've been thinking about her all day. About how her body felt under mine. And how damn sassy her mouth was when she ran away.

And now, here she is, with both surprise and interest in those stunning blue eyes that are so much like her uncle's, it's almost disconcerting.

Will doesn't look too surprised to see her as he shoves a cracker full of cheese and meat into his mouth. "I didn't realize you've met Ike before."

Her eyebrow rises. "We've met, but I didn't know his name."

"I knocked her right off her feet this morning. Stole the breath from her chest."

Will's eyes narrow on me, and she smirks.

"He knocked me down while I was running."

22

"By accident," I clarify immediately, holding up my hands. I'm a smart man and don't want to die today.

"This is my niece," Will says, his voice just a little harder than it was before. "Sophie."

"Pretty name." I hold my hand out for her to shake. Her eyes fall to my hand, and then lift to my face, and the confidence written all over her is just *daring* me to toss her onto a bed and have my way with her.

That, or I *really* irritate her.

Maybe both?

"So, if you're Ike, that must mean that you're Ike Harrison, quarterback extraordinaire."

I grin and clutch her hand in mine.

"Quarterback is close enough."

"I've seen you play, of course," Sophie says and tries to tug her hand free, but I keep hold of it just a second longer. "You have my hand."

"I know."

"Don't make me kill you." This comes from Will, who's still stuffing his mouth. "I actually *like* you."

"No offense intended." I step back and offer Sophie a smile. "I'm just glad I ran into you this morning."

"And why is that?" she asks. "So I could cushion your fall?"

"There is that," I concede. "I wouldn't want to be injured in the off-season. *Plus*, you gave me something to think about all day today."

"You're cute *and* sweet," Meg says with a grin. "You remind me of Will when he was your age."

23

"I'm still cute and sweet," Will objects. "Okay, Ike, grab some food and follow me before I have to kill you out of principle. Family honor and all."

I laugh and snag a couple of things from the spread on the counter and then follow Will outside where a couple of other players are playing Ping-Pong in a covered rec space.

"She's beautiful," I say when we sit, watching my teammates.

"Yep," is his only answer.

"Taken?"

His eyes narrow on me again.

"Come on, man. You know I'm not an asshole, like a lot of the guys on the team. Hell, I wouldn't trust her with those two over there, and I like them."

He sighs. "Not taken. But if I ever found out that you caused *one* fucking tear to fall from of her pretty blue eyes, I'll have your heart for breakfast."

"Naturally." I eat the last of my snack, happy with the turn my day just took.

"You're back under contract negotiations." The subject change is abrupt, but it's the main reason I came to talk to him. I'd like to hear his thoughts on this. "Or, about to be."

"Yeah, we should start the back-and-forth in the next couple of weeks." I sigh and push my hand through my hair. "It's damn nerve-racking."

"Why are you nervous? They'll renew your contract in a heartbeat. You're the new big thing in this league, and I can guarantee that Paddington won't let you leave any time soon. She's got her eye on a championship, and she knows that you're her ticket there. No owner is going to be stupid enough to trade you."

"They might not offer me enough money, and then I'll have to go somewhere else."

I didn't mean to say that part out loud. I want Will's advice, but no one knows that money is a concern for me regarding this new contract. Hell, thanks to my first contract, I'm a fucking millionaire.

Or, I *was*.

But that four-year contract is up, and it's time to renegotiate.

Will watches me for a long minute. "I know that rookie contracts aren't huge in the grand scheme of things, but you were drafted at number two, and I know you got a hell of a signing bonus. You didn't get peanuts, Ike."

"No. It was a good salary, especially for a farm boy from Oklahoma." I take a drink of the sweet tea that Meg offered me when I arrived. "More money than I thought I'd make in a lifetime."

"You're single, you're talented, and you're *not* injured. So, what's the problem?"

"Nothing. Forget it. It'll all work out. This isn't your problem, and I'm sorry I brought it up."

"Fuck that shit," he says, waving me off. "I brought it up. We're friends, and I was a young player once, too.

Tell me what's going on in that head of yours. Have you had one too many concussions?"

"I'm hesitant to say this out loud and jinx it, but I can report that, so far, that's never been an issue for me."

"Good. So, spill it."

I rub my hand over my mouth and watch Rogers taunt Malloney with the Ping-Pong paddle, and then I decide that Will's the one person in Seattle that I feel like I *can* confide in.

"Okay. So, yeah, it was a lot of money, like I said. But there are agent fees, taxes, all the damn things. And yeah, there's still plenty left over, but my family—"

I shake my head. I can't believe I'm voicing this out loud.

"How much?" he asks without looking over at me. "How much have they taken?"

"I bought a house here, paid off my sister's student loans, and most of the rest goes home."

Silence sits heavy around us until I finally give in and look his way. He looks damn pissed off.

"Why are you sending all of your money home?"

"My dad always used to say when I was in high school, *I can't wait for Ike to go pro so I can retire.*"

"How old is he?"

"Almost sixty, I guess."

"And you retired him."

I shrug. "Isn't that how it works? If a guy does well,

like *really* well, and his family has always struggled, he helps."

"Sure, he *helps*, Ike. He invests in the family business or pays off his parent's house or buys them a new car. Sends them on vacation once a year. He doesn't give everyone he knows a free ride while he worries about his own financial situation."

"I'm not worried," I insist. "I'm not. I don't have any debt, and I live just fine."

"Ike, football isn't like other professions. You'll play for another ten years. Twelve if you're *very* lucky and don't get injured or just age out. What then? You need to be planning for the future, not supporting everyone back home."

"Yeah, I know. I've thought of that. But if I'm offered the high end of what contracts are going for right now for star players, I'll be fine."

"Let me ask you this; are you okay with the amount of money that you send to your family?"

No. Absolutely not. I'm a damn ATM.

But instead, all I say is, "They're my family."

"Be careful with that," is all he says. "And regarding your contract, you have an excellent agent. I wouldn't worry about the negotiations. But if you have questions, you have my number."

But I *will* worry. Because it's important to my dad that they live a certain lifestyle.

And I'm expected to keep them in it.

"More sweet tea?"

I glance up and smile at Meg, who's the sweetest woman I've ever met. When she heard that I'm so far away from home, she made it clear that I'm welcome here at any time.

I don't take advantage of that, but it's nice to know that they're here if I need them.

And Will Montgomery has been my idol since I was a little kid. It's crazy to me that he's my friend now, too.

"Sure, thanks. Is Sophie still around?"

Meg laughs and tops off our glasses. "She went home, but she did reluctantly give me permission to give you her phone number if you asked for it."

"I'm askin'."

Sophie is smokin' hot, with curves for days and a quick wit.

Yeah, I'd like to get to know her better.

"Heart," Will whispers, and I grin at him.

"Not one tear will be shed."

"What did I miss?" Meg asks with a frown. "Did Will threaten you, Ike?"

"Every day, ma'am. It's just my everyday existence. My private cross to bear, if you will."

"Be nice to him." Meg narrows her eyes at her husband, winks at me, and then turns to walk back inside.

"You ratted me out."

"Dude, she's a *mom*. They know everything."

"Yeah." He blows out a breath. "You're not wrong about that."

THE GYM WAS my enemy tonight.

I work out twice a day, like clockwork, whether I'm in the off-season or prepping for a game that week. I have to stay conditioned.

I can't slack off, then have to try to get it back under control a month before training starts.

No way.

So, I jogged this morning and literally ran right into the delectable Sophie.

That was awesome. If I could, I'd arrange for that to happen every damn day.

But this evening, lifting weights was just a suck fest. I couldn't concentrate, and it didn't help that my dad called me four times in the middle of bench presses.

I let it go to voice mail each time.

And I could just hear the curses and frustration coming out of his mouth back home.

But for tonight, I just don't give a fuck.

I keep thinking about my conversation with Will and the look on his face when I told him that I send so much of my money home. Obviously, it's not as *normal* as my dad always made me think it is.

I even casually asked Rogers if he spoils his parents,

and he smirked, saying he paid off their house, and they wouldn't let him do anything else for them.

I don't mind helping my family. I want to make them as comfortable as I can, and I know that the extra money is a huge help.

But Dad takes advantage of me now, and it's only getting worse with time. He acts like because he encouraged me to play ball in middle school that he's the reason my career is doing so well.

It couldn't have anything at all to do with the fact that I work my ass off and have talent. No, it's all about him.

He thinks the money is never-ending. That it'll never go away.

And I just don't have the patience to talk to him tonight.

"You packing it in?" Rogers asks, out of breath from a round on the treadmill.

"Yeah, my head's not in it."

"You've seemed pissed since we left Will's place," he says and drinks out of his water bottle. "You guys fight or something?"

"Nah, nothing like that. Just family shit, man."

"Families can be a pain in the ass, that's for sure. Go home and shake it off. Tackle it again tomorrow."

"That's the plan. Have a good one."

I grab my bag and head out to my car, toss it into the backseat, and get in to drive home. Most of the guys live on the east side of town, near Lake Washington. It's a great neighborhood, but I wanted an ocean view, and I wanted to be on my own.

I love my team, but we're together a *lot.*

So, I found a house with a view of Puget Sound near Alki. I wonder if Sophie lives over that way, too. That would be convenient.

It's late evening as I drive through Seattle to get home, and it's almost dark when I pull into the garage.

I'm grateful that Pam, my housekeeper, was here today and left some lights on for me.

When I walk into the kitchen and smell something in the oven, my mouth immediately waters.

And sure enough, there's a note from Pam on the counter.

Ike,

I made you some chicken enchiladas. They're in the oven. Sour cream is in the fridge, and chips are in the pantry. You need more home-cooked meals!

Pam

I grin. Good ol' Pam. She's my mom's age and mothers me just as much. She's been with me since I bought this house three years ago and came highly recommended by my realtor.

She cleans once a week, and more often than not, leaves me food on her way out the door.

She's a gem.

Before I tear into the food, I hurry upstairs and take a quick shower to wash off the sweat from the gym, pull on some athletic shorts and a tank, then return to the kitchen to feast.

I don't even bother to put any of it on a plate. I just set the pan on the table, grab the sour cream and chips, noticing there's a jar of salsa, as well, and snag a fork on my way back to the spread on my table.

"I need to give Pam a raise," I decide as I take the first bite and sigh in happiness.

And my phone rings.

Dad.

"Nope." I shoot him to voice mail, but seconds later, a text comes through.

Dad: Stop whoring around long enough to answer the goddamn phone.

I roll my eyes and call him, putting him on speaker so I can keep eating.

"I was at the gym," I inform him with my mouth full when he answers. "What's up?"

"I went to the dealership to trade in my truck today, and the money wasn't there for it."

I sit back in my seat and scowl. "Dad, you just traded in your truck last year."

"That's not the point."

"I'm at the end of the contract," I remind him. "I don't have it to give you, Dad. You'll have to drive the old truck for another year."

"Bullshit. After all I've done for you, *now* you're going to be greedy?"

"You have *got* to be kidding me." The words are out

before I can stop them, and there's nothing but stunned silence on the other end of the line. "I'm not a kid, and I've given you more than most would. If that's not good enough for you, I don't know what to tell you. There won't be any more money until I know what's up with the negotiations."

"But, I have bills—"

"You shouldn't," I shoot back. "And if you do, that's not my problem."

I hang up and drop my head in my hands. Jesus Christ, I'm sick to death of being nickel-and-dimed by that man.

And my mom, although never asks for a thing, also won't stand up to my dad and tell him to stop.

Because she's afraid of him. She's always been afraid of the son of a bitch.

I'm not going to let him ruin these enchiladas.

I finish off the pan, then set it in the sink and walk into the living room to turn on ESPN, but now I can't stop thinking about Sophie and her sassy smile.

That gorgeous face is a much better place for my mind to wander to than thinking about my jerk of a father.

I have her number.

It's late, but it's not *that* late.

So, without giving it too much thought, I call her.

"I don't usually answer unknown numbers," is her answer.

"I don't blame you. I don't either. This is Ike, by the way."

"I hope so because otherwise, I'm hanging up."

"So, you were *hoping* I'd call?"

She scoffs, but I can hear the smile in her voice when she says, "I don't know about that. What are you doing?"

"I just ate a pan of enchiladas, and now I'm calling you. What are *you* doing?"

"You ate the *whole* pan?"

"Hell yeah. It was delicious."

"I'm actually a little jealous. I was just making a list of what I need to do for work tomorrow."

I scoot down on the couch, getting comfortable and enjoying the sound of her smoky voice. "What do you do for work?"

"You can google my name sometime. You'll find me. Mostly, I'm a nutrition coach and an influencer."

"Like, on social media?"

"Yes."

"That's pretty interesting. You'll have to tell me more about it sometime because I have no intention of googling you. I'd rather hear about you from *you*, Sophie."

"Suit yourself."

"I always do. Do you live in the Alki neighborhood?"

She pauses, and I smile.

"I'm just making conversation, not trying to be a

creeper or anything. And I'm hoping that you'll be running again so I can see you. Maybe we can even go for a run together."

"Does that mean that *you* live there?" she asks.

"Yep. Want my address? You can come over any time."

"I do want your address so I can sell it to all the groupies."

I smirk. "Bullshit. I know who your uncle is. You wouldn't do that."

She laughs, and it moves through me like good wine and leaves me just as high. "Okay, I wouldn't. No, I don't live over there, but I have family who do, and it's my favorite neighborhood to run in."

"Score one for me."

"Are you always a charmer, Ike?"

"I'm *never* charming. Hell, I wouldn't know the first thing about it. I just call it like I see it. And you're a beautiful woman that I'd like to get to know better. Go to dinner with me tomorrow."

"That wasn't a question."

I feel my lips tip up. "No, ma'am. Not a question."

"Do I hear a hint of a southern accent in your voice?"

"I'm from Oklahoma, but before I tell you any more about me, you have to go out with me."

"Hmm. Well, I *do* like the accent."

"Is that all you like?"

"Hmm," is all she says, and it makes me laugh.

"I'll pick you up at six."

"I'll pick *you* up," she says, surprising me. "I have to help my cousin with something tomorrow afternoon, so I'll already be in the 'hood."

"Okay, I can work with that. I'll text you my address."

"Great. Do I have to get dressed up?"

"I hope not." I laugh at that. "I'm a pretty casual guy."

"Okay. Well, then I guess I'll see you tomorrow."

"Sleep well, beautiful Sophie."

She's quiet for a moment and then whispers, "You, too," before hanging up.

My dad may have pissed me off, but I had a delicious dinner, and now, I have a date with a beautiful woman. Life's pretty fucking good.

CHAPTER 3

SOPHIE

"*I* think that's everything," Abby says as she nibbles on the end of her pen and reads through her notes.

Abby is in college to be a news reporter, and she asked if she could interview me for her class.

On camera.

This is actually good timing because I knew I'd put on a little makeup for my date with Ike anyway, so I'm killing two birds with one stone.

"Thanks for helping me with this," she continues. Abby is a gorgeous brunette with skin so smooth and clear that she practically glows. She's always been a little shy. Definitely soft-spoken.

So, I was completely and pleasantly surprised that, as soon as the camera came on, Abby smiled, and there was no evidence of the shy girl I'd known for so long.

"You're really good at this," I inform her as she

begins to put some of her things away. We're in the living room of the new house at the compound, and although she lives here, she stores all of her equipment in the storage space under the stairs to keep it out of the way. "Like, *really* good. Do you want to be an anchor at a news channel? Because you totally could."

"No." She shakes her head, but her lips tip up in a sweet smile. "I want to cover sports. ESPN, here I come."

I blink twice and then feel my heartbeat quicken. "That is *awesome!* I mean, you'll eventually have to move away, and that makes me sad, but what an incredible goal, Abs."

"It'll take a while. I'll probably have to start locally and work my way up. I'm not going to hide that Will is my uncle, but I'm not going to ride that coattail to get a job, either. So, we'll see."

"I'm in your corner," I assure her and glance over as Liam walks in from the kitchen.

"Oops, are you still filming? I can go."

"No, we're finished," Abby says. "But thanks for asking. Did you make that?"

She points to the muffin in his hand, and he grins at her.

"Nah, I stole it from the other house. Lucy's been baking this morning."

"Did you bring us some?" I ask my brother, and he just takes another bite and shakes his head. "Selfish."

"When it comes to baked goods, you bet your ass."

I laugh and then check the time. When Ike texted me his address, he told me to be there around 5:30 rather than 6:00, and if I'm walking, that means I have to go now.

"I'd better go."

"Oh, I'll drive you," Abby offers. "Since Maddie dropped you off earlier."

"Why don't you have your car?" Liam asks.

"Maddie asked me to go get pedicures, and we both know that I never turn that down, and then I had her drop me here for my interview with Abs. I have a date in a little while, and I'm just going to walk. No biggie."

Liam stops chewing. "A date with who?"

"I don't think you know him," I reply. "But he lives here in the neighborhood, so it's easy."

"I'll take you." Liam leaves no room for argument.

I shrug, rethinking the walk. I'd rather not arrive at Ike's all sweaty and out of breath.

That's not sexy.

"If you don't mind, I'll take the ride, Liam. Thanks again, Abby."

"No, thank *you*. I'll send you a link when it's live. Now, I'm gonna go see what else Lucy's been baking."

I follow Liam out to his car and lower myself into the passenger seat.

"Here's the address." I show him the screen of my phone. "It's not that far."

"Just a few blocks down and around the corner," he

39

confirms and starts his car. "How long have you known this guy?"

"About a day and a half."

His head whips around, and he pins me with a surprised look. "What? And you're going to his *house?*"

"Uncle Will knows him, *father.*"

"I'm not acting like Dad."

"Totally are. I should just call you Isaac."

"You're my only sister, and I'm looking out for you."

"And I appreciate it. I love you, too."

He pulls up into the gated driveway, and when we approach, the gate opens without us having to speak into the speaker thing.

"He's loaded," Liam says. "But that doesn't mean he's not a fucking creep."

I sigh and roll my eyes as he pulls up in front of the door, where Ike is already standing in the doorway.

"Is that Ike Harrison?"

"Yep." I offer him a fist bump, and then I step out of the car and smile at Ike. "Hey."

"Hey yourself." He watches with sober eyes as my brother heads down the driveway and disappears from sight. "Am I poaching on someone else's territory?"

"Huh?" I glance back at the empty drive and then back at Ike. "Oh, God. Ew."

A shudder runs through my body, and I shake my head.

"No, that's my *brother.* I was at his house this afternoon, and he dropped me off."

Ike physically relaxes and smiles at me. "Ah. Gotcha."

"Besides, if I had a boyfriend, I don't think he'd willingly drop me off at another man's house so I could go out to dinner with him."

"Hey, you never know. There are some odd people out there."

He gestures for me to follow him inside.

"Are we staying in for dinner?" I ask and take in his house as Ike shakes his head no. His home isn't enormous. In fact, it's just a normal-sized house, but it has a beautiful view of the water. "I like this a lot."

"Thanks." He grins and follows me to the windows. "I do, too. I knew I wanted a water view, and when this came up for sale, I snatched it. I had to install the gate, though."

"Smart idea. People got Will's address over the years, and having a gate kept out almost all of the crazies."

"Almost?" I glance up and see that he's raised an eyebrow at that. "Not all?"

"Most people are just curious, you know? They want a glimpse of where he lives, so they get as far as the gate and then turn around and leave. But once, a woman was *really* determined, and she got in somehow. I can't remember how because I was a teenager when it happened."

"I guess once out of all of these years isn't too bad of a record." He reaches up, as if he's done it a hundred times before, and tucks my dark hair behind my ear. "You look gorgeous, Sophie."

"Thank you. You're not too bad yourself."

That's the understatement of the millennia. He's just in jeans and a green long-sleeved Henley and Jordans. Completely casual.

But he's also just delicious.

I can't help but notice again just how freaking tall he is. And he's not lanky. Not at all. He's muscular, with broad shoulders, and the sleeves of the Henley are pulled up on his forearms, showing off the muscles and veins there, which cause every nerve ending in my body to sit up and begin to salivate.

"I hope you're hungry."

Hell yes, I'm hungry, and not necessarily for food. But that would sound entirely too forward.

So, I just smile. "Definitely. Where are we going?"

"Do you like seafood?"

"I do. I grew up in Seattle, where fresh seafood is a religion. How about you?"

"Well, I grew up in the middle of the country, where fresh seafood was a myth, but I've grown to love it since I've lived here. There's a place on the water called Salty's."

"I know it well. Great menu."

"Cool. Let's do it, then."

"I don't get a tour of your house?"

He grins as he grabs his keys and wallet off the kitchen counter. "I'm hoping that happens later."

"What if it doesn't?"

He simply shrugs. "Then it doesn't. No harm."

Yeah, I like him.

"Okay, let's go eat our weight in crab legs."

He grins and gestures for me to follow him into the attached garage where I find a sweet, brand-new black Toyota truck.

"Nice," I say with a grin as I buckle my seat belt.

"It was *free*," he says as he starts the engine. "Can you believe it? They put my face on a billboard and gave me a free truck. Said I could lease a new one for as long as I play here."

"That's fantastic." I turn on the heated seat. "Sponsorships rock, don't they? Uncle Will always gets free stuff."

"I wasn't expecting it," he says, shaking his head as he heads down the driveway and through the gate. "I mean, I knew that it was possible, but I didn't expect it so soon."

"From what I've read and heard, you're excellent," I reply. "Very talented, well-liked, and you're handsome. It doesn't surprise me at all that you were offered things right away."

"So, you think I'm handsome."

I smirk. "Yeah, yeah, you know you're good-looking."

He laughs and pulls into Salty's parking lot, and once he's parked, he holds up a hand.

"Stay put."

No man has ever made sure I stayed where I am so he can circle around and open my door for me.

It's kind of nice. And it reminds me of my own parents, and that makes me a little sentimental.

Ike opens my door and offers his hand to help me out of the truck, then locks the vehicle as we walk to the door of the restaurant, and he opens that one for me, too.

"There are two of us," he tells the host, who consults something on his podium, then grabs a couple of menus and shows us to a table against the windows that face the water and the skyline of Seattle.

The sun is just starting to set, casting the water and the buildings in pink.

"That's beautiful," I murmur.

"Gorgeous."

I glance over and find him looking at me rather than the view, and I wrinkle my nose at him.

"Do you come here a lot?" I ask as I sip some water.

"A couple of times a month," he replies. "Not too often. How about you?"

"I like to cook," I reply, and we're interrupted by the waitress, who takes our orders and then walks away, even though it's clear by the look on her face that she knows who Ike is.

She doesn't make a fuss.

It's just one more reason why I love this place.

"So, you like to cook," he prompts me.

"I do. I cook a lot for my job, and I usually eat the leftovers from that."

"You said you're a nutritionist?" He drinks his own water. He didn't order any alcohol with his dinner. I don't know if that's because *I* didn't or if he just doesn't drink.

"Yeah, I'm all about eating healthy but also sensibly. So many fad diets just aren't sustainable, but if I can teach people how to make good choices with everyday foods, that's what really helps. I also share my shopping lists and even do some videos in the store so I can show how to choose your food."

"That's actually really awesome. I've never thought of grocery shopping like that."

"Have you always been lean?"

"Sure." He nods thoughtfully. "I've always attributed that to being so active and having a killer metabolism. Genetics, too, I guess."

I lean in, enjoying this conversation. "Many of us weren't as lucky. And there are just far too many people out there with body dysmorphia, who may also have eating disorders, and that can be deadly. I know all too well."

His eyes narrow on me. "Tell me how you know."

I love the way he watches me with those killer brown eyes. The way he *listens.* He's not just placating me, having a surface conversation so he can get in my pants later.

He's interested in what I'm saying.

And, in my experience, that doesn't happen often. It's sexy as hell.

"I had a best friend in middle school who was just a tiny little thing. Super skinny and petite. And I was in such a horrible phase with my body. Hormones were kicking in on overdrive. I was changing, and you know how some kids get that, well, chubby look to them? I don't mean that in a mean way, I'm just—"

"I get it," he says with a nod and butters a hot roll that was just delivered, then offers it to me.

I bite in and sigh in happiness.

"Anyway, that was me. And I thought I'd be like that forever, and I was *not* happy with it. I told Steph about how I was feeling, and she said, *Oh, that's easy.* And proceeded to coach me on throwing up what I ate, like she did."

"Oh, shit," he whispers.

"Yeah, oh, shit. I don't know how long she'd been doing that, but I suspect a long while. I did it for a couple of months, and the two of us had a sort of new club. We were excited. We kept a journal, and we had the best buddy system ever.

"Until she died. She was thirteen, and her heart gave out from lack of potassium, which I now know is common in those who suffer from bulimia. I went to college to learn about nutrition and eating disorders, and I knew that I wanted to help people who suffered from them. I've never intentionally thrown up since then. And yes, I'm naturally curvy, but I'm also tall. I'm not built to be small, and I'm totally okay with that."

"Honey, your curves are *kickin'*."

I grin at him. "I know. Now I do, anyway. I have no body issues at all. But back then, I was just a kid who didn't want to be different. Not to mention, I grew up in the Montgomery family. We're chocked full of gorgeous famous people. And it's easy to be hard on yourself when you don't see yourself in the same light. Mom and Dad got me counseling, and I'm fine."

I sit back and blow out a breath.

"Wow, that was a lot of baggage to unpack on you on the first date."

He smiles, and his eyes are full of so much kindness, it puts butterflies in my belly.

"I can handle a little baggage," he says. "I have strong shoulders."

Our meals are delivered, and when we're alone again, he taps his fingers on the table.

"Question," he says.

"Shoot."

"Is this a healthy dinner? Like, am I blowing it up here?"

I take in his crab, shrimp, and potatoes with a salad, and shake my head.

"No, it looks great to me. I'm eating the same, minus the shrimp."

"But, there's butter."

I grin at him. "And thank all the gods for it. What's seafood without butter? It's all in moderation, Ike."

He nods in agreement and pops a potato into his mouth.

"I couldn't agree more."

"Okay, that's enough about me for now. Tell me about you. All I know is that you play football—quite well, at that—and you're from Oklahoma."

"I mean, that's pretty much it in a nutshell."

I lick my buttery lips and shake my head at him. "Nope. That's not even scratching the surface. Siblings?"

"One sister. She's a teacher."

"Parents still alive?"

"Yep, and still married."

"If you hadn't played pro ball, what would you have done?"

He goes very still, and I worry that I just asked the wrong question. But then he clears his throat.

"I probably would have ended up working on the family farm until I either died or my body gave out on me."

The humor and fun banter from a minute ago is gone, and I can see that this is a sore spot for him.

"Football sounds like much more fun," I say, trying to lighten the mood again, and he smiles now, his shoulders relaxing.

He doesn't like to talk about home.

And that's okay. We don't have to.

"Have you been to Pike Place Market and the first Starbucks yet?"

He sips his water. "No, actually. I keep meaning to, but life's just busy, you know?"

"Yeah, I get it. But, you live here now. You have to see it. They have the *best* tiny donuts ever, and they throw fish. It's really something to see."

"Great. When are you taking me?"

I can't help the grin that spreads over my face. "Tomorrow's Thursday, so it shouldn't be too busy. Do you already have plans?"

"Any plans can be changed for you, sweetheart."

"Okay, then. I live not far from there, so you can meet me at my place this time, and we'll go from my condo."

"I know we're still on this date," he says as he pulls some meat out of his crab leg. "But I can't wait for the next one."

"Are you sure you don't know how charming you are?"

He just smiles, and I laugh.

"That's what I thought. You totally know. But I like it, so it's okay."

He makes me laugh throughout dinner, and when I suggest we share a key lime tart, he agrees.

And holds my hand while we eat it.

I've never been the touchy-feely type. Not that I don't like affection, but I'm not needy. I don't need someone constantly touching me, and I'm not a huge hugger.

And yet, I'm already addicted to Ike's hands.

His tucking my hair behind my ear, and holding my hand here, only makes me want more.

Much more.

But I haven't decided if I'm going to give him more tonight. Or offer it.

Because it's the first date, and Aunt Meg has always preached the value of the three-date rule.

It worked for her and Uncle Will.

"What's going through that gorgeous head?" Ike asks.

"I'm wondering if I'm going to get that tour of your house."

It's sort of the truth.

"If you want it, you got it."

"Yeah." I finish the last bite of the tart. "I definitely want it."

I don't know what I'll do when we make it to the bedroom, but I'll play it by ear.

Because I'm absolutely not ready to go home.

CHAPTER 4

IKE

I pull back into my driveway and then walk around the truck to let Sophie out. She slides to the ground, a soft smile on her lips, and doesn't take her hand from mine as we walk inside.

Suddenly, she stops short and almost pulls me to the ground.

"Shit."

"What?" I quickly look around, trying to spot any sign of danger. "What is it? Call 9-1-1."

"No. No, it's not that. But, please, for the love of all that's holy, tell me that your name isn't Isaac."

"We were formally introduced yesterday, sweetheart. I'm *Ike.* Nice to meet you."

She blinks at me and swallows hard, and I can see that my joke is lost on her.

"What's your *full* name?"

"Isaiah Matthew Harrison, at your service."

"Oh, thank God." She clutches her chest and seems to have to catch her breath. I'm surprised her legs don't give out on her.

"Do I need to take you to the emergency room?" I press the back of my hand against her forehead. "You don't seem feverish."

"No." She laughs now and holds on to my arms as she shakes her head. I admit, I like being this close to her.

I like it a lot.

"Sorry, my dad's name is Isaac, and it occurred to me that Ike might be short for Isaac, and that made me panic a little."

"Because it would be weird," I finish for her.

"Kind of, yeah. Okay, a lot. It would be a lot weird for me."

"Well, you can breathe easy."

She sighs, then takes in my house the same way that she did earlier. With interest and clear appreciation.

"Did I mention that I really like your house?"

"You might have. What is it about this place that appeals to you?"

She taps her finger on her chin as she walks through the kitchen to the living room, near the wide windows that give me a full, clear view of the water.

"It's so open," she says at last. "And I know most homes *are* open, but this isn't a new house, and that's unusual."

"Built in 1936," I confirm. "But it's been through

some renovations over the years. Opening up the kitchen to the living room happened about ten years ago, I think."

"It's perfect. And these windows just make it seem bigger. It's just cozy. And welcoming. No bad vibes here."

"That's a relief." I shove my hands into my pockets because everything in me wants to pull her close and feast on her lips. "It's not a big house."

"It doesn't need to be," she says immediately. "Trust me, there are houses of all sizes in my family, and at the end of the day, it's the people *in* them that make them a home. Not the size."

"How big was the house you grew up in?" I ask.

"About this size," she says, thinking it over. "My dad builds houses for a living. He and Mom bought a place just before I was born. He completely renovated it and made it what she wanted. They still live there."

"I like that," I decide with a nod. "Want to see the rest?"

"I thought you'd never ask. Let's go, tour guide."

I grin and take her hand in mine, then lead her down a hallway. "There are two bedrooms and a bathroom over here. I use one for a guest room and one for a home gym."

"I like it." She takes in both rooms and nods thoughtfully. "You utilized the space well for the gym."

"It's not a big room, so I called in a professional to make the most of it. Let's go upstairs."

I walk ahead of her and glance back just in time to see her eyes pinned to my ass.

"It's just *right there,*" she says, gesturing to said ass. "I can't help but stare at it."

"Of course, you can't help it."

"It's a hardship," she insists, but then laughs when I tug her to the top of the steps and lightly smack her own behind. "Oh, I like this a *lot.* I don't think I'd ever leave this space."

I have to admit, the loft is awesome. I have a big TV set up, with deep-cushioned couches, blankets, and everything that a person could want for a lazy afternoon.

"I have the gym." I glance around with a nod. "And I needed a place to veg out, as well. It's all about balance."

"For sure."

I lead her to my bedroom, and she glances around, nodding in satisfaction. "Nice."

We share a glance.

Yeah, the sexual tension is there.

I want to toss her onto that bed.

And it's going to happen. Sooner or later.

"What else?" She turns to me, hands on her hips.

"Just a game room."

"A *game* room?" She tilts her head to the side in interest. "Show me."

I gesture for her to follow me to the other side of the house, but stop before opening the door.

"Is there a secret knock or something?" she asks when I pause. "It doesn't say *No Girls Allowed.*"

I lean in to kiss her nose, unable to resist her. "No. This room is over the garage, and it's big. It used to be used as an office space, but I don't have a need for that. I'm fine with my laptop on the dining room table."

"Okay."

"The thing you need to know about this room is that it's all about competition. There's no mercy shown in here. You play to win. Sometimes, there's bloodshed."

Her eyebrows wing up in surprise.

"So, just a regular family dinner with the Montgomerys." She snorts. "Let me see. You're killing me here."

I step back and open the door, watching as her eyes widen. Her jaw drops, and she slowly walks through the door.

"This looks like something out of a movie." It's a whisper as she moves through the room. There's another TV used exclusively for video games. I have a pool table, an air hockey table, and a small basketball goal set up with a wide net, like something at a carnival.

But it's what's in the corner that catches her attention.

"You have a *vintage* pinball machine."

"I do. Indiana Jones from 1993. My mom might slap me for calling that vintage."

Sophie grins and pushes on the paddle buttons. "Does it work?"

"Of course, it does." I plug it in, and it lights up, bells ring, and a ball appears, ready for play.

"Before I begin," she says, turning to me, "I want to set some ground rules."

"But this is *my* machine. My machine, my rules."

She narrows her eyes. "I'm the guest."

"Let me hear your rules."

"Okay. Actually, there's really only one rule."

"And that is?"

"If I win, I get your football jersey."

"Which one?"

She rolls her eyes. "Your *Seattle* jersey."

I have a million of them. That's no hardship.

"And if I win?"

"You won't."

I move in closer to her, tuck her hair behind her ear, and press my lips there. "I don't think I've told you how much your confidence turns me on, sweetheart. It's sexy as hell. But I'm damn good at this game, so tell me what I get if I win."

She clears her throat, and it makes me smile.

"What do you want?"

You. Naked. Beneath me.

But instead of saying that out loud, I simply smile. "I want you to cook for me."

She blinks in surprise. "That's it?"

"You said you like to cook, and that's what I want when I win. And I'm warning you, I eat a lot."

"Done. Easy. Okay." She rubs her hands together, hops on her toes, and shakes out her shoulders, rotating her head from side to side as if she's a fighter getting ready for a match. "Are we going to bust out a practice round?"

"Absolutely not."

Her smile is quick and fierce.

God, I freaking adore her.

"Who's up first?" she asks.

"You said it yourself. You're the guest. So, by all means…"

I step around the machine so I can watch her face as she assumes the position.

She pulls back on the lever and sends the ball flying through the machine. Those baby blues are wide and focused as she watches the metal sphere dance and bounce, and then she hits it when it comes her way.

She's good. Better than good, really.

"Someone in your family has one of these," I guess.

"A few of the uncles do," she confirms. "I'm not kidding when I tell you that I'm in a family of grown-up kids. It's pretty fun."

She almost misses a hit and shakes her head.

"Stop talking to me. You won't make me lose by distracting me."

"I'm just making friendly conversation."

"No, you're not." Her lips twitch.

"You know, you could work on your stance." I move behind her and let my hands brush her sides, then down to her hips. I nudge the inside of her ankles, so she widens her feet. "You have to have a strong foundation for this."

"I know exactly what you're trying to do." She wiggles her butt against me, and I'm instantly rock-hard. "And two can play at that game."

"That's a whole different game, honey." I lean in and kiss her temple, brushing my lips down her ear. "One that I'm all too happy to play with you."

The ball falls down into the hole, and she's finished with that first round.

"Damn, you made me lose the first ball."

"I'm just trying to help."

A new ball bounces into the slot, but before she can play it, she turns to face me, presses her breasts against my chest, and tips up her chin so she's looking me in the eye.

"Do you play dirty when it comes to football, too?"

My gaze falls to her lips.

"I never play dirty. I just get the job done."

She walks her fingers up my arm to my shoulder and then slides them into my hair and pushes closer against me.

"Ike."

"Hmm."

"I'm going to win this game whether your hands are on me or off of me."

"You can try."

With glittering eyes, she turns back to the machine, and I take a step away so I can watch her work the ball and paddles.

I'm hard as can be, ready to take her right here, and she's cool and collected, playing an excellent game.

I have to admire her for it.

And when she's finished with the third ball, her score is damn respectable.

"Your turn," she purrs with a satisfied grin. "What's in the fridge over there?"

"Drinks. Help yourself. Grab me a Pepsi, if you don't mind."

"I don't mind." She returns with a bottle of cola for me and fizzy water for herself. "I have a personal question."

"Okay." I pull back on the lever and send the ball flying. "Shoot."

"Do you ever drink alcohol?"

"Not really. I don't have anything against it. I just personally think it's a waste of calories. And my dad has drunk beer forever and has the gut that goes with it. No thanks. Not to mention, I need a clear head for my job."

She watches quietly as I play the game, and I do quite well until the ball falls through a hole that sends it out of the game.

"What about you?" I ask her as I send the next ball into play.

"Not often. Like you, it's calories that I'd rather eat than drink. But, about once a month or so, we have a cousins' night get-together at the compound, and I'll have a drink or two there."

"Compound?"

"Yeah." I hear her take a swig of her drink. "It's two houses side by side that my family owns, and a bunch of the cousins live in them together. It's the Montgomery compound, or that's what we call it. It's totally extra, but it's safe, and all the uncles are big proponents of safety."

"Did you live there?"

"No." She sips again. "They didn't turn it into what it is now until this past year when they bought the second house. I never lived in the first one. But I visit often. That's where I was earlier today."

"So, your brother lives there."

She doesn't answer right away, and I risk taking my eyes off the ball to look at her.

"You paid attention."

"Hell yes. I notice everything about you."

She's quiet again as I finish out the game, and when it's all said and done, I'm surprised to find that I lost.

I lost.

That doesn't usually happen.

"Holy shit," she says in surprise. "I won. I WON!"

She starts to do the victory dance, and I can't help but grin as I watch her shake her ass in celebration.

"Okay, pay up, Harrison. Where's my jersey?"

"You stay here, and I'll get it."

She smiles and bites her lower lip, and it takes everything in me to walk away from her.

Jesus, I haven't wanted a woman like this in a long time.

I choose a jersey out of my closet and then return to the game room to find Sophie exactly where I left her, waiting.

"Here you go. One football jersey." I pass it to her, and without missing a beat, she whips the sweater she's wearing over her head and tosses it onto a chair.

She's not naked beneath the sweater.

She's wearing a little pink tank that hugs her like a second skin. Instinctively, I take a step toward her.

Sophie smiles and tugs my jersey over her head. The neck is so wide on her, it falls off one shoulder, showing me a pink strap and lots of smooth skin that I'd like to sink my teeth into.

"Fits like a glove," she declares.

Without thinking, I advance on her, boost her onto the pinball machine, and with her face cupped in my hands, I kiss the hell out of her.

Her full lips are soft and hungry as she gives as good as she takes. She nibbles on my bottom lip, then surrenders as I sink into her and explore her mouth.

One hand journeys under the jersey to cup her breast, and she moans. When I tug on her nipple with my thumb and forefinger, she gasps and raises her legs up high on my hips in invitation.

"I want you so badly that I ache with it," I groan against her neck.

And when she doesn't answer, I pull back to look into her eyes.

The lust is there, but it's the hint of uncertainty that has me stepping completely away from her.

"I won't do anything you're not okay with."

"You didn't," she rushes to assure me, shaking her head as she swallows hard. "Trust me, I was on the same page."

"But you're not ready for anything else right now."

She looks like she wants to say something, but then she just offers me a forced smile. "I'm sorry."

"Why are you *sorry*?"

"Well, if you think I was teasing you or something—"

"Whoa." I hold up my hands, stopping her. "Honey, I'm fine. You don't need to apologize for anything. I'm just happy to be here with you. I'm not a jerk who thinks that a woman can't set boundaries. Please, set them. And be clear about them so I don't have to read your mind. I'm all for that. I'm a shitty mind reader."

Her smile turns genuine now, and she reaches out to tug me back to her.

"Let me clarify. I think you're sexy." Her voice doesn't tremble in the least, and I feel like we're back on sure footing. "And funny. And super nice, which I wasn't expecting, although I don't know why I wasn't expecting it. I just wasn't."

"I'm not that nice. Nice guys finish last, so let's forget that part, okay?"

She chuckles. "And I'm absofreakinglutely attracted to you."

"Good. I didn't fuck this up. Same goes."

I brush my nose against hers and feel her exhale in relief.

"But we don't have to rush the physical stuff, right?"

"Nope. No rush. We can wait, like, ten minutes. Twenty if you really need it."

She laughs again and shakes her head at me. "Yeah, the sense of humor gets me."

"What? It's not my firm chin line? My rock-hard abs?"

"I haven't seen the abs." She stills my hands before I can pull up my shirt. "But I'm sure they're lovely."

"Yeah. Lovely is the word I'd use."

"I can't wait to see them, but for tonight, I think kissing is the right place to stop."

"I can live with that. Happily. And I mean that."

"And *that* is why you're a nice guy."

"Take it back." I narrow my eyes, giving her a mock glare, and she just laughs.

"Nope. Leaving it out there. And I'll tell you a secret." She crooks her finger, inviting me to get even closer, and this time, she presses her lips to *my* ear. "I don't care what other women think, Ike. *I* find kindness to be incredibly sexy."

I pull back far enough to see her once more, and

this time, I kiss her on the forehead, just breathing her in.

"One day, I hope I get to make love to you while you're wearing just this jersey."

Her eyes widen, and I grin.

"Nice guys have dirty desires, too, you know."

"I should hope so." She laughs and hops off the pinball machine. "I should get home. I have to work before our day date tomorrow. I just have to call an Uber."

"Hell no. I'll drive you."

"I'm in the city," she says. "You don't have to drive me all that way. I can easily call a car."

"I can drive you," I insist. "Besides, I need to know where to pick you up tomorrow, anyway. It's no trouble."

"Are you sure?"

"Come on. Maybe I'll get a tour of *your* house."

"It's a condo."

"Shouldn't take long, then." I follow Sophie through my house and out to the garage, then open the truck door for her.

"Ike."

"Yeah?" I lean in and fasten her seat belt for her.

"Thanks for everything tonight. I had a lot of fun."

"I don't remember the last time I had that much fun," I agree and kiss her cheek. "And you're welcome."

CHAPTER 5

SOPHIE

*H*e never left.

Ike brought me home, and I invited him up to my place so I could give him a tour, and we ended up on the couch with hot tea and talked for hours.

Then, in the middle of me telling him about how I had to take my high school SATs twice, he fell asleep.

Just drifted right off.

So, I covered him with a blanket and went to bed.

Standing in my living room, both hands full, I simply stare at the big man that I've quickly come to like very much, and grin.

At some point during the wee hours of the morning, he lay down fully on the couch and tucked the blanket firmly around him. Just before I walk over to wake him, Ike's eyes flutter open, and he blinks when he sees me.

"Is this a dream?"

"Nope." I walk over as he sits up, and I offer him a green smoothie. He scowls.

"What the hell is this?"

"Your daily allowance of greens," I inform him as he takes the glass, and I sip my coffee.

"Why do *you* get coffee?"

"Because I already drank my smoothie. Now, be a good boy, and you, too, may have some coffee."

He eyes me with distrust over the rim of the glass as he takes a sip and then scowls. "Mmm, so earthy."

"It's really good for you. I'm surprised you don't drink these. Uncle Will told me that most of the players do."

"They do," he says after gulping down three-quarters of it. "Doesn't make it taste any better."

"It's not *that* bad." I sit next to him and sip my coffee. "How did you sleep?"

"Like a rock. I could always sleep anywhere." He finishes the glass, then takes it into the kitchen and rinses it out in the sink, sets it in the dishwasher, and helps himself to coffee.

It doesn't offend me in the least that he's making himself at home in my condo. In fact, I like it.

"You have a lot of filming equipment in here," he says, eyeing my tripod, lights, and the small microphone I usually wear that's sitting on the counter.

"As I told you, I film a lot of cooking and shopping

videos for my followers. It's just me here, so I leave the equipment set up. It's easier."

"I can see that. What was the last thing you cooked?"

"The charcuterie spread that I took over to Uncle Will's the day I saw you there was the last filming day. We did a few days' worth of videos, so I'd have content all week."

"Who's *we?*"

He sips out of his mug. His brown hair is all in disarray, and I'd like to push my fingers through it.

"My assistant, Becs, and I. She comes over a couple of times a week. She also edits all the videos and gets them ready for posting, and she handles most of the website and social media stuff. She's a gem and a single mom, so having a flexible schedule works out for her."

I keep babbling, and he keeps listening, but all I can think is, is this technically still date number one, or are we on to date number two?

Because I'm trying *really* hard to follow Meg's three-date rule before sleeping with someone, but damn, it's hard.

It's especially hard when he looks like *that.* All rumpled from sleep, with bare feet, standing in my kitchen just casually drinking my coffee, as if we do this all the freaking time. All I can concentrate on is what those abs *really* look like under his white T-shirt.

I'm quite sure they're way better than *lovely.*

"Sophie."

I blink and try to act nonchalant. "What's that?"

"I asked where you went. You stopped talking and got lost in a stare."

Yeah, I was staring at his freaking *abs*.

"Oh, sorry. Coffee hasn't kicked in yet."

I stand and move to walk around him so I can pour another cup, even though I *never* drink more than one cup of coffee a day, but he catches my elbow and tugs me to him, sets both of our mugs aside, and just pulls me in for a great big hug.

Instinctively, I circle my arms around his middle and hold on just as tightly and breathe him in. He's hard, but not uncomfortably so. In fact, I think I could stand here, just like this, all day long.

"Oh, this is nice."

"Hmm." He buries his nose in the top of my head and kisses me there. "Good mornin', beautiful."

"Mornin'."

It's a long hug. In some circumstances, it could slide right over into awkward.

But I'm not feeling uncomfortable at all. In fact, the longer it goes, the more relaxed I become.

"If you continue to snuggle me like this, I might fall asleep."

I feel him smile against the crown of my head, and then he lets me go.

"Would you rather I make you breakfast," I offer as I continue around the island to the coffee maker, "or would you like to just grab something down at the market? There are some cute restaurants down there."

"Let's do that," he says. "As long as you aren't offended by me wearing the same thing today as I did last night, I won't go home and change."

"You're not stinky," I inform him with a wrinkle of my nose. "It's fine with me."

Deciding against more coffee, I set the mug in the dishwasher.

"I'll be ready in ten. I have an extra toothbrush you can use."

"I'd appreciate that," he says with a nod and follows me back to my bedroom, walking straight into the en suite bathroom.

From the closet, I hear the water come on, and I smile. I've only lived in this condo for about a year, and Ike is the first man I've brought back here. I've been so busy with work, I just haven't had time to date.

But I like having him here.

I've just pulled on a cardigan when the man himself appears in the doorway. He straightened out his hair a bit, and he looks as fresh as he did when I first arrived at his house yesterday.

"How do guys do that?" I ask, gesturing to him.

"Do what?"

"Look like *that*. If I had to regroup with the same outfit from the day before, I'd look homeless."

"Doubt it," he says, shaking his head. "You're freaking gorgeous, Soph. Can I call you Soph?"

I grin. "Yeah. You can. Come on, I have so much to show you today."

"Lead the way."

～

"It's good that I had a big breakfast before you introduced me to the tiny donuts," Ike decides as we walk past the flying fish counter at the market. We each have a small bag of the hot, fresh goodness, and we're munching away. "Otherwise, I'd not only eat this whole bag but some of yours, too."

"I'll have plenty left over," I reply with a shrug. "I take them home and warm them up in the air fryer, then serve them with a small scoop of ice cream. It's especially good when I'm on my period."

My eyes widen, and I immediately wish the ground would open up and suck me down.

"Uh, that was probably too much information."

"Not at all. Now I know what to do when Aunt Flow comes to town."

My gaze whips up to his, and he grins, wiping a few grains of sugar from the corner of my lips, then licks his finger.

"Hey, Ike!"

We turn at his name being called out, and it's fascinating to watch the change on Ike's face.

He goes from warm affection to cold politeness in the blink of an eye.

"Hey, man," Ike says to the fan.

"Oh, my God, I always hoped I'd run into you," the guy says with enthusiasm and shakes Ike's hand. "Hey, can I get a picture?"

"Sure," Ike says.

I discreetly take the bag of donuts from him and stand aside while he signs a few autographs and poses for photos as a small crowd gathers around him.

He's not rude to one person. Not even the woman who wants to cling to him a little too much.

He simply disengages from her and sets her aside.

"Okay, everyone, thanks for all of your support, but I'm going to get on with my day now. Y'all have a good one."

He waves and takes my hand, and without a pause, leads me away from the crowd that continues to form.

"That doesn't happen often," he says when we're out of earshot of the fans. "But all it takes is for one person to recognize me, and then it's all downhill from there."

"I get it," I assure him. "It doesn't bother me. I'm really used to it. I have a lot of celebrities in my family."

"Yeah, well, I don't love it. I don't mind—that's not it. I really do appreciate the fans and love how enthusiastic they are about football. They're my people, you know?"

"Sure."

"But sometimes, they get a little overzealous."

"Has it ever gotten scary?"

His grip on my hand firms as we cross a busy street, headed for my condo.

"No, there is usually security around. And like I said, I'm rarely recognized when I'm alone. I think people expect to always see me with my teammates."

"That makes sense. I'm glad the little crowd gathered when we were at the end of this little date."

"Me, too."

He walks me into my building and escorts me up to the condo.

Once I open the door, he pins me against the door frame and kisses me in that way he does that makes my toes curl and my belly do back flips.

"When can I see you again?" he whispers.

I lick my lips, still tasting him there, and try to think straight.

"I have a family thing tomorrow," I reply. "So, the day after?"

"I'll text you," he promises, then kisses my forehead and backs away. "Have a good day, Soph."

"You too, Ike."

I smile and close the door, then lean against it and let out a long sigh.

Saying I *like* Ike is a severe understatement.

But I do. I like him a lot.

~

"THERE'S A BUBBLY BAR," I say with a giggle as I walk into Luke and Natalie's house with my mom. "With the most beautiful balloons I've ever seen."

"The whole place is gorgeous," Mom agrees, and is suddenly swept up in a big hug by Natalie herself. "Hello, mother of the bride."

"Oh, stop," Nat says, shaking her head. "You'll make me start crying again. My baby's getting married. How is that even possible?"

"Well, a hot movie star swept her off of her feet, and now they're getting hitched," I reply. "I think that's the same story as yours."

Nat laughs and then nods. "True enough. Come on, you two. Help yourselves to the mimosa bar and the food spread in the dining room. We couldn't decide on just one thing to serve, so there's a huge buffet. And Nic brought all kinds of cupcakes and macaroons, too."

"No one will ever go hungry at a Montgomery function," I say with a laugh. "I'm going to go say hi to the bride."

I leave them and cross to where Liv and Stella, her cousin *and* bestie, are huddled around the bubbly bar.

"Leave it to you to throw a wedding in less than a month."

Liv spins around, shrieks in excitement, and throws her arms around my neck to hug me.

"Geez, how many drinks have you already had?"

"Just one. I'm just so *happy*, you know? All of the

girls in the family are here, and we get to eat all the good things and talk, and it's just the best."

"Don't forget about the karaoke," Stella says smugly. "Because we're going to crush that shit."

"Also, don't forget about the presents," I remind her. "I brought you something *good.*"

"No one needs to get me anything," she insists, but her eyes drift to the gift table. "What is it?"

"You'll see later." I kiss her cheek, and then the front door opens, and there's more commotion as even more moms and cousins arrive. "How does Alecia seem to age backward, even with a teenager *and* a business to run?"

"She's a vampire," Stella says with a laugh.

We're all swallowed up in hugs and excitement, as if we don't see each other on the regular.

In fact, we just all had our monthly birthday dinner at Sam and Leo's house two weeks ago.

There are so many people in this family, and therefore birthdays, that we just have one celebration a month. It totally works for us.

But no matter how long it's been since we've seen each other, whether a couple of weeks or just a few days, we're always excited to be together.

I know that not all families feel this way, so I never take it for granted.

"I had a dream last night," Olivia's youngest sister, Chelsea, says. "I met Chris Evans at the supermarket. He was trying to pick out some radishes, so I helped him, and there was this immediate attraction between us."

"Of course, there was," Stella says with a smile.

"But then he said," Chelsea continues, "I guess looks don't matter. It's the inside that counts. And then he took my hand, and we left the store together. And what I want to know is, does Chris Evans think I'm *ugly*?"

"Of course not," Aunt Nic says. "You're a beautiful girl."

"But he said—"

"In a *dream*," I remind her. "Not real life."

"Have you ever met Chris Evans?" Zoey asks.

"Well, no. But I'd like to."

"He's, like, more than twenty years older than you," Haley reminds her.

"If it's Chris Evans, there's nothing wrong with that," Chelsea replies, her nose in the air.

"Whoa." Natalie holds up her hands as the rest of us laugh our heads off. "Do *not* let your father hear you say that."

"No kidding. You forget that you live in a family where meeting celebrities is a very real possibility." This comes from Sam, who's pointing her finger at her niece. "Your sister wanted to meet one of the Jonas brothers when she was twelve, and your uncle Leo was ready to make it happen."

"I'm still mad that Dad said no," Haley replies with a pout.

I move over to where Meg's laughing with my aunt

Brynna, and lean in to whisper to her. "Can I talk to you for a minute?"

"Of course."

I lead her down the hall to a restroom and close the door behind us.

"What is it? What's wrong? Are you hurt?"

Meg grabs my shoulders in her hands, worry all over her pretty face, and I shake my head.

"No, no, I'm fine. Really, perfectly fine. I just have a question for you." I take a deep breath, let it out slowly, and then purge the story as fast as I can. "Okay, so I went on a date with Ike last night, and then he took me home, and he ended up staying over because he fell asleep, and then today, we went on another date, but he didn't go home between dates, and I don't know if that was one date or two, and I'm *really* hoping you'll tell me that it was two dates."

She blinks. "That was a crazy run-on sentence. Also, awww! You're following the three-date rule!"

"And it's killing me, so please tell me that was two dates."

"Well, did you sleep in there somewhere?"

"Yes. He slept on the couch, and I slept in my bed."

She nods, thinking it over. "I'm going to say it was two dates. You slept separately and went on two different dates on two separate days."

"Yes!" I jump up and down and clap my hands. "Thank God."

"I can see where Ike would be hard to resist. He's adorable."

"He's hot as fuck, Aunt Meg. And he's so freaking nice, I can't even stand it. But I'm gonna hang in there for one more date because I don't want to take it too fast."

"I think that's smart."

"But...do I have to wait for a few days *after* the third date, or, like, can we go on the third date, and then when he takes me home, I can jump him?"

"I think at that point, it's just semantics," she says with a smile. "You're a grown woman in your late twenties, and you can decide for yourself when you're ready to sleep with a hot-as-fuck man."

I press my hand to my mouth and then laugh. "Are all quarterbacks hot?"

"I seem to think so, yes." She smiles and tucks my hair behind my ear the way my own mother would. "I'm here if you have questions. Not about the sex," she says quickly. "But about life with a professional football player. Because as exciting as it can be, it's not all championships and roses."

"I know. I get it."

"I think out of most of the women in the world, you do. You have the benefit of being in this particular family. That will come in handy."

"Thanks." I hug her tight and then open the door of the bathroom, where I find Liv, Stella, and several others with their ears pressed to the wood. "What the hell?"

"You're dating Ike Harrison?" Liv demands. "When were you going to tell the rest of us?"

"Well, right now, actually. You're a bunch of nosy women."

"Of course, we are," Stella says. "Also? Ike is hot with a capital H."

"I know. But I'm holding out on the sexy stuff until after the third date."

"How many dates have you been on?" Liv wants to know.

"Two."

They all look at each other and then at me.

"Call him. Call him *right now.*"

I laugh, despite wanting to do just that. "First, I want to enjoy this party with you guys. We'll eat, drink, and make wedding gowns out of toilet paper."

"Liv doesn't get to play that one," Abby says, speaking up for the first time. "She's a seamstress for a living. She'll win."

"She's the mannequin," Stella announces. "Come on and grab a roll of Charmin."

CHAPTER 6

IKE

"Coach Mac wants to see you, man."

Rogers leans into the locker room, delivers the message, and then pops out again. We're at the training center today, going over some theory, watching film from last year, and just keeping our heads in the game.

The off-season isn't always easy. It's sometimes a challenge to make sure you don't get out of shape and to make sure that you stay on the same page as your teammates.

The majority of us choose to live and stay in Seattle so we can work out together and meet like this regularly. Not all teams do, but this is how we run our team, and I'm grateful.

Besides, I'm never going back to Oklahoma. Not if I can help it.

I grab my bag out of my locker and walk down the

hall to where Coach keeps his office. He could have a fancy office somewhere else, but he likes to be close to the team.

"You wanted to see me, Coach?"

"Hey, Ike." He shuffles some papers on his desk, then gestures to the seat across from him. "Why don't you close the door."

"Uh, sure." I do as he asks and then sit across from him. "Why do I feel like I've been sent to the principal's office?"

He sighs, swears under his breath, and looks generally irritated. He's a big man with broad shoulders and meaty hands, and he's old enough to be my father. And today, his jaw is set, and the lines on his face seem to be more pronounced than usual.

Yeah, Coach is pissed off.

"Look, I'm going to start by saying that I don't give a rat's ass what you do when you're not on the job with me. I couldn't care less."

I narrow my eyes. "Okay."

He blows out another breath. "Are you seeing Will Montgomery's niece? I think her name's Sophie?"

"Why do you ask?" I don't mean to sound defensive, but this is a ridiculous question. On second thought, yeah. I'm defensive.

"Like I said, I don't care. Go out and fuck everyone if you want to, as long as it's consensual and you don't get fucking sued for it. But I've been instructed to ask you, which is also a bunch of BS, if you're having an affair with Sophie Montgomery."

"I've been on exactly two dates with her," I reply stiffly. "And I plan to continue seeing her."

He nods, and his face looks grave, the way it does when he knows we're going to lose a game.

"That's what I figured."

"What's the problem, Coach?"

"I don't know the whole story here. It sounds like someone took a picture of you with Sophie yesterday, and it's in the media."

"Okay. I'm high profile, and she's the same, so that doesn't really surprise me."

"Apparently, Florence isn't too fond of the Montgomery family right now."

I lean forward. "Coach, Will works with us a lot. He's been a part of this organization in one form or another for decades."

"I know." He holds up his hands. "I know all too well. There's been a lawsuit against Florence filed by another of Will's nieces, a Stella McKenna, and some bad press in general. Florence wants to distance us from that whole family, and she wasn't pleased at all when she saw the photo of you with Sophie."

"Too fucking bad."

Coach nods gravely. "I figured that would be your response. Hell, it would be mine, too. No one can dictate who you see in your private life, Ike. Not even Florence."

"Then why are we having this conversation?"

"Because you're about to go back to negotiations for your contract," he says easily. "And if that bitch decides to make life hard on you out of spite, she certainly can. Now, I won't let her trade you without putting up one hell of a fight. You're the best quarterback I've seen on this field since Will was here himself, and that's saying a lot."

"I appreciate it."

"I'm just letting you know that this could make trouble for you. And before you say it, no. It's not fair. But Florence isn't known for being fair; she's known for being ruthless."

"Did she ask you to talk to me about this, or is this you looking out for me?"

"Both," he says without hesitation. "It's pretty shitty that she put me in this situation, but it's both. Because I won't lose you to a petty grudge that woman's carrying."

"What do you suggest I do?"

"Live your life. I'm not going to tell you to stop seeing her because I can see by the look on your face that you'll tell me to go fuck myself."

"Maybe not in those exact words."

"Until your contract is solid, just don't flaunt who you're dating in the media and under Florence's nose. That's all."

"Thanks for the heads-up."

I stand to leave.

"Ike."

I turn back to him. "Yeah?"

"Don't worry about this, but don't blow it off, either. That's the bottom line."

"Thanks, Coach."

I walk out, but I hear him mutter under his breath, "Bunch of bullshit."

He's right, it *is* a bunch of bullshit. But I've seen what Florence can do when she's mad at a player. She has a god complex, and she can be *mean.*

But I won't stop seeing Sophie just because Florence has a grudge and a mean streak. Not in this or any other lifetime.

"YOU KNOW, I never thought I'd see the day when Seattle's star player came into my shelter to help out with the animals."

I glance up to see Rhonda standing in the doorway of the cat room, leaning her shoulder against the doorjamb.

"I like animals," I reply.

"But you won't let us put you in our advertising or the media. You just come in here, clean up literal crap, and then go home."

I shrug and pet little Maggie the calico before I close her pen door and move on to the next one to clean the litter and tidy the kennel. I like animals, and I enjoy spending time here, helping out every week. Sometimes these cats and dogs go a long while without being loved on, and that makes me feel bad.

"I don't need the recognition to do this," I reply softly. "And if I could adopt them all, I would."

"I know. Me, too. Have you been over to see Buster yet?"

"Not yet. I'm taking him on a walk when I'm finished in here."

Rhonda nods and licks her lips. "This will be your last walk with Buster, Ike. He's been adopted."

I feel my stomach drop. Not because I don't want the sweet Great Dane to have a permanent home, but because I wish that I could be the one to take him.

It just wouldn't be fair to an animal. I'm gone too much during the season, and I'm single. I can't just leave them.

"Wow. Well, good for him."

"I know you have a soft spot for that horse of a dog, and I wanted to let you know."

"Yeah, thanks." I nod and offer her a tight smile before she leaves the room, and I turn back to the cat kennels.

Well, damn.

I always save my time with Buster for last so I can take him on a nice, long walk and play with him, tucker him out a bit. He's a big boy at only two years old, and he has so much energy. Way too much for the little attention he gets in this place.

But now, he'll go home with someone, and hopefully get all the attention in the world with a big yard to run around in. That's awesome for him.

And I'm a selfish ass for feeling sorry for myself.

After some kitten cuddles, I finish in the cat room and make my way over to the dogs. I purposely start on the opposite end of the room from Buster and take my time cleaning out each cage, sitting and petting each dog. One little pug was surrendered when her human passed away, and she's been especially sad, so I hold her and give her plenty of lap time before I move on to the next cage.

Finally, I stop at Buster's kennel and grin at him. When he's on all fours, he hits me right at the hip. And when he jumps up to kiss me, he's taller than my six-foot-five.

"Hey, you massive baby." With his whole body wiggling in excitement, Buster rushes over to greet me and almost takes me to the ground. "Yeah, I missed you, too. I hear you get to go home to a family later today. Are you excited? You should be."

I rub his dark face, kiss his head, and get to work cleaning out his pen before I clip a leash to his harness and take him out for our walk.

Buster's great on the leash and is excellent at not pulling me around. At some point in his young life, someone took the time to train him well. I take my time with him today, enjoying each moment with him.

"Be good," I tell him and grin when he cocks his

head to the side, listening. "You're getting out of this joint and going to a whole new life. You be a good boy in your new home, you hear?"

He licks my whole face in one big swoop, making me laugh.

"Yeah, I love you, too. Take care, big guy."

I finish the last of my chores and poke my head into Rhonda's office before I leave.

"Have a good week, Rhonda."

"You too, Ike. Thanks for your help."

I nod and leave the shelter, get in my truck, and head home for a shower. It's been a *weird* fucking day.

I know that I don't want to be alone, and with Sophie at her family thing today, I decide to call a couple of friends over to blow off some steam in the game room.

Rogers and Malloney are always up for hanging out. They're also both single and usually available on short notice.

"We're in," Rogers says when I call him. "We're just leaving the training center. We'll head your way."

"See you soon."

I hang up as I pull into the garage and immediately head up for a shower to wash off my morning workout and all the dog and cat hair that clings to me every time I'm at the shelter.

By the time I'm done and dressed, the doorbell rings.

"Good timing," I mutter as I open the front door to see the guys standing there, boxes of pizza in hand.

"We brought sustenance," Malloney announces. "I'm going to cream you two at air hockey today."

"You wish," Rogers says as we walk upstairs to the game room. "You're horrible at air hockey."

"Fuck that noise." Malloney scowls and opens the first box of pizza and takes a bite. "Why does Harrison look like his mother just died?"

"Huh? I do not."

"You kind of do, man. Did Sophie already dump you?"

"No. Wait, how do you know I'm dating her?"

"Dude, we all know." Malloney just winks at me, and I let out a sigh.

"Did you get into some shit in Coach's office?" Rogers asks.

"No, just politics bullshit." It's not a lie.

"There's always some of that," Malloney agrees. "Not usually in the off-season, but there's always some shit floating around."

"Yeah, well, it's fine."

We eat and then play, and to our surprise, Malloney does indeed kick our asses at air hockey.

"Have you been practicing?" I ask him.

"I'm a natural," he says with a cool shrug. "You assholes just underestimate me."

Rogers rolls his eyes just as my phone rings.

"You guys go ahead and play; I gotta take this."

I walk out of the playroom and take Sophie's call.

"Hey, beautiful."

"Hi." I can hear commotion and laughter in the background. "Hey there."

I grin. "Are you still at the party?"

"Yeah. 'Salmost over, though."

"You've been drinking."

"They have the *cutest* mimosa bar I've ever seen. Might have had a couple."

She sounds ridiculously adorable when she's hammered.

"What can I do for you, Soph?"

"Need you to come get me. I can't drive."

I frown. "Someone there should be able to give you a ride. Or is everyone drunk as hell?"

"No, they could, but I don't want them." She takes a breath. "Want *you*. And if you pick me up, it's considered the third date, and then I can jump you."

I feel my eyes go wide. "Excuse me?"

"Third date," she repeats. "I'll text you the address."

She giggles and then hangs up, and a few seconds later, a text comes through from her.

Sure enough, there's the address.

I didn't know that we were waiting for three dates in order for her to jump me, but I'm not about to argue.

I hurry back into the game room and announce, "You have to leave."

My friends both blink at me. "What?"

"You have to go. Sorry, I have to go get Sophie."

"Is she okay?" Malloney asks.

"Fine. Drunk. Needs me to get her. You have to go."

"We don't mind waiting for you," Rogers says, but then sees the look on my face, and he laughs. "He's trying to get laid."

"That's none of your business."

"Say no more," Malloney says as he grabs his jacket. "Have fun. Be safe. Wear a condom."

"Thanks for the stellar advice."

They're both snickering like middle school boys when they leave out the front door, and then I make a beeline for my truck, plug the address into my maps, and head out.

To my surprise, she isn't too far away from me. Just a few miles. So, it doesn't take long for me to arrive at a gated home also on the water.

I push the buzzer, and the gate immediately opens for me. I can't see the house from the gate, but when I turn a corner, it comes into view, and I whistle long and low.

"Nice digs," I mutter as I pull up in front of the house.

Sophie's not out front, so I decide to ring the doorbell.

And when I do, the door is flung open, and I find Meg grinning at me. "You came!"

"That's what he said," I hear from someone inside, followed by all kinds of laughter.

"I'm not sure if I should have. It sounds like this is a girls-only party."

Meg just shakes her head and pulls me through the door. Sure enough, there are at least two dozen women inside, in various states of intoxication.

"Sophie called," I say lamely.

"I'm here!" I see a hand go up in the middle of the crowd and wave around. "I'm coming!"

"And if all goes well," a brunette mutters, "she'll be saying that again in a few hours."

I'm not easily embarrassed, and I'm not embarrassed now.

I'd say I'm intrigued.

And mildly turned on.

Sophie jumps up and comes staggering my way.

"Hey, I'm surprised to see you," she says, making the others laugh.

"Really? Because you called and asked for a ride home."

"I'm trying to sound nonchalant," she says in a loud whisper. "So I don't sound too needy."

I tuck her hair behind her ear and grin down at her. God, she's fucking adorable.

"And are you needy, Sophie?"

"Maybe. But I'm not going to tell *you* that. Also, you're really hot. Why are you so hot?"

"Just good genes, I guess."

"Really good," she agrees.

"Hey, Soph, aren't you going to introduce us to your friend?"

Sophie's eyes go wide, and then she turns to the others. "You can *see* him?"

I'm laughing now, unable to help myself.

"He's not a figment of your imagination," Meg says with a chuckle.

"Right. Oh, right," Sophie replies. "Everyone, this is Ike. He plays football, and he tried to kill me in the park."

"That's so romantic," a blonde says with a deep sigh. "I wish that would happen to me."

"That's my cousin, Zoey," Sophie informs me. "I can't tell you everyone's names because you'll never remember them."

"I'm Stella," another blonde says with a grin. "And this gorgeous woman is Olivia. She's the one getting married."

"Congratulations," I say with a nod.

"Stella's getting married, too!" someone calls out. "But that's a party for another day."

"We should go," Sophie tells me and tries to muscle me back to the door, but she's so drunk that she's as weak as a baby bird. "Wow, you're strong."

"You're drunk," I reply and simply lift her into my arms.

"Awww!" is the collective response from the hoard of women in the room.

"Be nice to my baby," a woman says and glares at

me. "If you hurt her, my husband and all of his brothers will hunt you down."

"That's my mommy," Sophie says with a loopy smile. "Love you, Mom. And you should really be worried about *him*, not me."

"Atta girl!" Stella calls out, and I walk to the door that Meg's holding open for us.

"Have fun," she says with a wink. "But not too much fun."

"All the fun," Sophie says and rests her head on my shoulder. "Bye, Meg."

I get her out to the truck and buckled in before I circle around to get in beside her. When I glance at the house, the front door is still open, and about a dozen female faces smile out at me.

"Bye!" They wave enthusiastically, and I wave back before driving away.

"Well, that was an experience."

"Pretty normal for us," she says and smiles over at me. "Thanks for coming to get me."

"It's no trouble at all. And you need to explain what you meant by this being our third date."

"Well, you picked me up, so it's technically a date."

"Okay."

"And that makes it our *third* date."

"Sure, I follow that."

"And after the third date is when I get to get you naked and have my way with you, and I didn't want to wait any longer."

CHAPTER 7

SOPHIE

I really need to shut the hell up, but when I'm drunk, I have loose lips. I always have. I overshare way too much.

And right now, the world is starting to spin, and that's never a good sign.

"How can I be so drunk after only *two* glasses of mimosas?" I brace my head in my hand, willing the world to stop spinning.

"You don't usually drink," he reminds me and reaches over to take the other hand in his, lifts it to his lips, and kisses me.

I sigh in a big, fat swoon and glance his way.

"I didn't eat a ton either," I murmur and watch his lips as they pucker again, and he plants them on another part of my hand. "You have really great lips, Isaiah Harrison."

"Yeah?" His eyes leave the road long enough to

glance at me and grin. "Just wait. You're going to *worship* my lips before long. Would you like me to take you to your condo? Or to my place?"

"I think we'd better go to your place since it's closer."

"Are you starting to feel a little sick?"

"Pssh." I try to blow off that idea, but the truth is that yes, I *am* feeling a little nauseous. I do *not* want to throw up, especially since I called Ike to come get me, and I plan to have the best sex of my life tonight. "Of course not."

"You might look a little pale, sweetheart."

I swallow and feel my palms clam up. "I *refuse* to be sick from two little glasses of champagne. It's just not going to happen."

But by the time Ike pulls into his garage, I feel *awful.* Thankfully, he's a gentleman and helps me out of his truck and into the house.

"I have bad news," I say meekly, but he just shakes his head and plants a kiss on the top of my head as he guides me inside.

"No way. No bad news. We're going to pour you into bed so you can sleep this off, and then we'll revisit naked time. No hard feelings here at all."

"Are you sure?"

"Don't be silly. You're here, in my house, and I'm putting you in *my* bed. I'm still the winner here."

"You're so—"

"If you say *nice*," he says, his voice just a little harder than I've heard it before as he presses his lips to my ear, "I'll spank your perfect ass, Sophie."

I know I'm drunk, but that makes me pause. "Well, then. Okay. Remind me to say *nice* when I'm sober."

He chuckles and helps me up the stairs, steers me to his bedroom, and as I sit on the side of his bed, he rifles through his dresser and comes out with a T-shirt.

"As sexy as you are in that outfit, you'll sleep better in this."

"Yeah." I stand and begin to yank off my jeans, not self-conscious at all. "I can't sleep in jeans and lace. Talk about uncomfortable."

With the jeans thrown on a chair in the corner, I reach for the hem of my shirt and hear Ike hiss between his teeth.

I turn to find him watching me with hot eyes and realize that I've been stripping down right in front of him.

"Oh, sorry. I'm so sorry. My brain is just foggy, and I kind of forgot that you were standing there, not that I care if you see me naked because that's kind of the point, but I'm not a tease, and—"

"Stop." It's that same firm voice from a minute ago that makes everything in me tingle. "You're fine, Soph. Get comfortable, okay?"

"Okay." I whip my top over my head, then quickly pull on his T-shirt, then wiggle out of my bra and pull it through the armhole before collapsing onto the bed. "If the room would just stop spinning, I'd be fine.

Totally fine. If you want to go ahead and do it anyway, I think it would be okay."

I hear him snicker, and then he's beside me on the bed, tucking me under the covers, and presses a tender kiss to my cheek that makes me tingle in a nice way.

"The first time I'm inside you, hell, *any time* I'm inside you, will not be just *okay*. If it's okay, I'm not doing my job. Get some rest."

I can't open my eyes, but my phone chimes next to my head on the nightstand.

Blindly, I reach out for it, but then I hear Ike's voice.

"This is Sophie's phone. No, she can't come to the phone. Hi, Liv. How many drinks did you give her, anyway? *Five*? She said two."

He laughs, but he sounds kind of far away.

"Oh, yeah, I'm sure she'll need her purse. She's at my house tonight, and I'm not too far from where the party was. I can swing over tomorrow and grab it for her. Oh, okay. No worries. I'll tell her. Thanks. And congratulations."

The bed moves as Ike sets the phone beside me, and then he kisses my cheek again and presses his lips to my ear, the way he did earlier, and my tingles have tingles.

"Liv called. You forgot your purse."

"Yeah. She won't steal my identity."

He smiles against my skin, and it makes my arms break out in goose bumps. If this is my reaction to him when I'm drunk and disorderly, I can't wait to see how I feel when I have all my faculties.

"No. She won't."

I snuggle down and turn toward him. "Thanks for this, by the way."

"You're welcome." It's a whisper, just before he kisses my forehead. "Sleep."

Since I can't do much of anything else, I do as he says, and let myself slip into sleep.

I SMELL COFFEE.

It's not the kind of smell where it's coming from far away, either. It's in this room. Near me.

But I live alone, and I didn't make myself any coffee.

Hell, I haven't even opened my eyes because my head is pounding with the beat of a thousand drums, and I think I might be dying.

It's a real possibility.

But then someone kisses my forehead, and last night comes back vividly into my mind, and I moan.

"Good morning." It's a whisper, but it feels like he screamed it into my ear.

"Ouch."

"I thought you might have a headache. Champagne always does that. I have coffee here for you, and some ibuprofen."

"Why are you yelling?"

I risk my head exploding and flutter my eyes open, just to immediately shut them again in defense against the bright light coming in through the window. I turn my face into my pillow and will myself to just die. It would be easiest for everyone.

"Come on, baby. Let's get you feeling better."

Ike pulls me onto my back, and with my eyes still firmly closed, I manage to sit up and lean against Ike's headboard, then sigh when he presses a mug of hot coffee into my hands.

"I really should drink a green smoothie first," I mutter, but take a sip of the coffee and sigh. "But this is so good. Tastes like heaven. Thank you."

"I don't have any green smoothies on hand," he replies. I feel him push his hands into my hair, brush it back over my shoulder, and some of the tension eases out of my shoulders. "But I can make you some eggs if you want."

I sigh and risk opening one eye. He's sitting on the edge of the bed, watching me with those eyes that I constantly seem to lose myself in. So kind. So sweet.

And so freaking sexy.

Of course, it would be *my* luck that instead of being sexy and alluring, seducing him with my charm, I called him while I was drunk off my ass and pretty much made him come get me and then proceeded to act like a complete idiot.

Then, I fell asleep—thank the baby Jesus and all the

baby apostles that I didn't throw up—and neither of us actually got any of the sex.

So, he had to take care of an obnoxiously intoxicated woman and didn't get any of the benefits.

"I'll be out of your hair soon," I say, still trying to be quiet so I don't do permanent damage to my brain. "I'm really sorry about last night."

"I didn't say anything about you being in my hair," he replies, but I just take another gulp of coffee, willing it to kick in quickly.

"I can walk back to Aunt Nat's house to get my car."

"Why would you do that?"

I try to shrug, but that's a bad idea. "Damn, how much did I drink?"

"A lot." He brushes his fingers down my cheek. "You drank a *lot*."

"It didn't feel like it," I admit and rub my hands over my eyes. Jesus, I'm still wearing my makeup. I can only imagine how awful I must look. "I guess it's true what they say. Time flies when you're having fun. They just need to add that you lose track of how much you're drinking."

"You were having a good time with people you trust. Nothing wrong with that."

I look at him now and try to offer a smile. "Thanks for everything. I'm sure it wasn't much fun for you."

"Actually, it was damn entertaining. Much more than it would have been to watch Rogers and Malloney play air hockey."

"You were with your friends?" I stare at him in horror. "Of course, you were. You have a life, too. You don't just wait around for me. Shit, I'm sorry, Ike. I'll grab my stuff and leave you be."

"Whoa." He catches my elbow when I move to get out of bed. "Did I ever give you the impression that I'm irritated or angry by the situation?"

"No, I just feel so awful. And I must *look* horrible, and I'm just so damn embarrassed."

I drop my face into my hands and wish the bed would open up and swallow me whole.

"Okay, first things first. We're going to make you feel better. I think a nice, hot shower will help, and here's some ibuprofen to help take care of the headache that the coffee didn't get rid of."

"I can go home—"

"Stop." And just like that, last night comes back into focus, and I remember him using that same tone with me. The tone that says, *I'm in charge here, and you'll fucking mind me.*

Not in a parental way.

In an alpha male way.

And I'll be damned if it's not the sexiest thing I've ever heard. I've never been one to enjoy following orders. I'm a Montgomery, after all. But for Ike? Yeah, I think I want to follow some orders.

"You're going to take a shower and get comfortable, then we'll talk."

"Okay."

I want to ask questions. Like, how does a guy who seems so laid-back and who is so incredibly kind and funny, also have this side to him?

And is it just with *me*, or is it all the time?

But he's right. First, I need a shower. My face feels awful with last night's makeup, and the hot water will help clear the cobwebs.

I follow him into his beautiful bathroom and stand aside as he gets the water going for me, and before he leaves the room, he pulls me in for a big hug. I cuddle up against his hard chest, and he brushes his hands up and down my back, which just feels so *good*.

After a long moment, when the water begins to steam up the room, he kisses the top of my head.

"Get in, and I'll set some clean clothes on the counter for you. They'll be too big, but they'll be clean."

"Thank you."

He leaves and closes the door behind him, and I strip out of his T-shirt and my panties before stepping into the shower that's big enough for most of the offensive line on the football team and sighing in appreciation.

Yeah, that feels damn good.

I just stand here and let the water stream over my head and down my body, then take a long, deep breath. If I'm going to be mortified, at least I'll feel clean and more in my right mind when I'm sent on my way.

I hear the door open, feet shuffling, and then the

door closes again, and I decide I best get busy cleaning myself up.

I use his shampoo and smile. It smells like him, which, of course, makes sense. I'm surprised to find that he has some nice face cleanser, so I use that, as well, and after a while, I'm feeling human again. Clean. Fresh.

And ready to face the music.

So, I dry myself off and dress in the clean T-shirt he left for me, but I avoid his boxers and sweats. Instead, I decide to forgo the dirty underwear and just slip on my jeans.

I can change into normal clothes when I get home.

"Thanks for the loaner," I say when I find Ike in the kitchen, sipping a cup of coffee. He looks over, narrows his eyes, and they travel down the length of me. "I'll be sure to wash it and get it back to you."

"No rush," he replies. "Were the sweats way too big?"

"Probably, but I just put these on. They'll be fine until I get back home and change."

"So, let me ask you a question." He walks around the island, sets his mug aside, and cups my face and part of my neck in his big hand. "Why are you in such a hurry to leave?"

My mouth opens, but then I immediately close it again, trying to gather my thoughts.

"Are you embarrassed?"

"Of course, I'm embarrassed!" That came out

quicker and way harsher than I intended, but I can't help it. I step away from him and pace his kitchen. "I called you last night, completely wasted, and practically threw myself at you. I'm no better than the groupies who follow the team around."

His jaw tightens, but I keep going.

"And I promised you all this great sex, but I was so sick from drinking too much that I passed out on you, and you had no choice but to pour me into your own bed and practically babysit me. It's not sexy, it's mortifying, and it would probably be best if I just got my stuff, what little of it there is, and left. We can just forget it ever happened."

"So, are you *always* completely in control, so that when you lose the slightest bit of that control, you react this way?"

I tilt my head, watching him. "Are you a therapist?"

"No, I'm genuinely curious. Because you didn't do anything wrong. We haven't known each other long, but we're definitely attracted to each other. Your call was fun and cute, and I thought you were a funny drunk. Not a jerk. Not promiscuous. Too much champagne makes me sick, too, so I don't drink it. And if I didn't want you in *my* bed, I would have just taken you home last night. So, I'm going to ask you what I did earlier. Do I seem mad?"

"There were a couple of moments when your voice got hard. And that's new, so I thought maybe you were trying to keep your temper in check or something. Even though it was kind of hot."

His eyebrow wings up in surprise after the last sentence.

"My voice gets hard when I'm fucking turned on, Soph."

I swallow hard. "Oh. So, are you bossy in bed?"

"Yeah. I am."

I nod slowly, absorbing this news.

"I'm sorry if you thought I was mad."

"I don't know what I thought." I shrug one shoulder, and then he advances toward me, picks me up, and takes me into the living room, settling on the couch with me in his lap. "Sick of the kitchen?"

His lips twitch into a smile. "That was just awkward, and this is more comfortable. We've established that no one is angry, so there's no need to be embarrassed, and I'm completely taken with you."

I loop my arms around his neck and settle in, feeling *way* more at ease.

"You forgot one part."

"What's that?"

"I'm obsessed with you, too."

He brushes the backs of his fingers down my cheek. "Well, that's handy. Because if you were revolted, we'd have to end things. That's the only right thing to do."

"You've got a point. Am I too heavy for you?"

"I outweigh you by a good eighty pounds, sweetheart. I'm fine."

"That doesn't mean I'm not heavy."

"Are you always argumentative when you're hungover?"

I laugh now and lean my forehead against his. "I don't know. It doesn't happen often."

"Okay, I think we need a reset. We're just going to sit here, with you *in my lap*, and just be for a few minutes."

"I mean, it's nice, but don't you have things—"

"I'm going to spank you."

I feel my eyes go wide, and then I bite my lower lip, and his gaze falls to my mouth. "I see you don't hate that idea."

"I don't hate it."

"Just settle in and reset," he urges. "Relax for a few minutes."

I rest my head on his chest and do as he asks. We breathe in unison, in and out, and I can almost hear our hearts beating in the same rhythm.

He's not just a goofy, nice guy.

There are so many facets to him that I don't even know yet. And, I want to know them. I want to learn everything I can about him.

And yes, I want to have sex with him. More than I want just about anything else.

"You're thinking too hard," he whispers, making me smile.

"My brain never shuts off," I admit.

"Never?"

I shake my head no.

"I bet there are some things I can think of to help you empty that busy mind of yours."

"I mean, you can try. Are you going to hypnotize me?"

Suddenly, I'm lying flat on my back, length-wise, on the couch, and Ike is hovering over me.

"No. I'm going to fuck you."

CHAPTER 8

IKE

Those sexy-as-hell blue eyes widen as she bites that lower lip, and I know everything I need to know with that one look.

"God, I fucking love the way you feel under me," I whisper as I move in to brush my nose over hers.

"We do seem to *fit*, don't we?"

"In more ways than one." I nibble my way over to her ear, then down to her neck, and she gasps as my teeth sink into the soft flesh of her shoulder. "Ah, you like that."

"What is it about the neck?"

I run my tongue over the spot I just bit and gather the shirt she borrowed from me in my hands, preparing to guide it over her head.

"Ike?"

I immediately pull back in case she wants to end this, but she's grinning. "Yeah?"

"I'm ready to see your abs now."

I feel the smile spread as I reach over my shoulder and tug off my shirt, toss it aside, and watch as her eyes, bright with lust and hunger, journey down my torso.

She reaches out and brushes her fingers over my stomach. "Yeah. I was right. They're lovely."

Her eyes find mine now, and she smirks.

"Like, *really* lovely."

Before I lower myself onto her again, I pull her up to a sitting position so I can discard her shirt, and when she lies back down, I feel my heart catch. It literally stumbles in my chest as I take her in. I've never seen anything like her in my life.

"Jesus H. Christ, Sophie, you're fucking beautiful."

Her pink bra is all lace and hugs her full breasts beautifully, but it can't hide her hard nipples.

And when she takes a deep breath, her throat works as she swallows hard, and I know without a doubt that I need to have my mouth on her.

And so I do. I kiss her lips and her cheeks, then work my way down once more to her neck and chest. Her bra is fastened with a clasp in the front—thank all the gods—and with the flick of my fingers, I...get nowhere.

Sophie lets out a breathless laugh. "It's tricky."

"I've got it." And after several seconds of fiddling with it, and only swearing under my breath once, I do.

The lace cups fall to the side, and I'm holding the softest skin I've ever touched in my hands.

"God, you have good hands." Her voice is still breathy, and her hips shift in anticipation as I graze my thumbs over her tight nipples.

"Why do you work so hard at covering these up?" I ask.

"Uh, it's illegal to walk around with them just out there for all to see." She licks her lips, and I can't resist reaching up to brush a thumb across that lower lip. And when she sticks her pink tongue out and licks my thumb, my cock grows even harder.

I didn't know that was possible.

"I mean, whenever I see you, you have these bound up tight."

"Clearly, you've never had large breasts, Ike. If they're *not* secure, bad things can happen. Black eyes. Strangulation."

I laugh now and cover her sassy mouth with mine, content to kiss the fuck out of her while my hands explore her torso, from those gorgeous tits to her ribs and stomach.

Until I just can't stand it anymore, and I unfasten her jeans.

She lifts her hips helpfully, and I slide them down her legs, tug them over her feet, and toss them aside.

"You're not wearing underwear."

"They were dirty." She reaches for me, but I pull back out of her grasp. "Come back here."

"Oh, I plan to. In a minute. I'm memorizing you."

She narrows her eyes but doesn't move to cover up. I fucking *love* how confident she is in her body. As if every curve wasn't already sexy as hell, the confidence only amps up the hotness level by about a hundred.

"Are you done yet?"

"No." I pull one foot up and kiss the ball, just under her big toe. She smells like my soap, and it does things to me. "I like your feet."

"I'm super relieved that you talked me into that shower and that it's a clean foot," she says, and then gasps when I plant my teeth on her toe. "That hurts *and* tickles at the same time. How is that possible?"

I just grin and leave wet kisses up her arch to her heel. And when I start to work my way up the inside of her leg, she sighs and begins to shift again, as if she just can't sit still while my mouth is on her.

And that's just fine by me.

Her inner thighs are just as soft as her breasts and just as sensitive. When I lick that crease, right next to her glistening pussy, she just about comes right off my sofa.

"I'm not even at the promised land yet."

Her hands reach out, and she fists them in my hair. "Oh, you're there. You're *right there.*"

Since waiting would just be mean, I lap her up, from her pussy to her clit, and Sophie moans, then mutters, "Ah, fuck. Fuck, fuck, fuck."

"That's right." Her lips are already swollen and slick, just begging for me to pull them into my mouth and gently pulse around them. She arches her back, and I know she's already *so close* to coming, and I'm not about to stop her.

I slide my tongue up to her clit and push a finger inside her, just as she falls over that glorious cliff, and her muscles convulse around me.

Jesus, I've never wanted to be inside someone as badly as I do right this minute. My cock is rock-hard, with a heartbeat of its own, but it's going to have to wait just a few more minutes.

Because I'm not finished with this yet.

"Ike."

She's chanting my name, either in a plea or a prayer, I'm not sure, but it's music to my ears. So when I add a second finger inside of her and lick my way up to her breasts, then pull a nipple into my mouth, she cries out. Her hands are fisted, one in my hair and one in my couch, and every muscle in her perfect body is engaged.

"Ike," she says and swallows hard. "Ike. Need you inside me."

"Go over once more first."

She thrashes her head from side to side. "Inside me, Ike. *Now*, damn it."

I press my lips against her ear. "Come, baby. Give me one more."

With a choked sob, I feel her tighten again as another orgasm moves through her. When her body calms, I pick her up and carry her up the stairs to my bedroom.

"Am I floating?" she asks, and I grin.

"We're headed to the bedroom because that's where the condoms are. But trust me, I'll be stashing them all over my fucking house from now on."

"Good plan."

I gently set her on the bed, yank out the box of condoms from the nightstand, pull out a few, and toss them onto the bed before quickly discarding my jeans.

But when I join her, before I can slide right inside of her, she boosts herself up onto her knees and pushes me down onto my back, gripping my cock.

"My turn."

The pleased grin on that stunning face is at once alluring and terrifying.

"Be gentle."

She laughs, and then I'm thrown right into the lake of fire. Because I'm 100 percent certain that I'm headed to hell, thanks to the thoughts running through my mind right now.

Her mouth is hot and just the perfect size to sink down over me, then firms as she pulls up.

I do *not* want to come in her mouth. Not this time, at least. So, when I just can't take it anymore, I take her shoulders in my hands and pull her off of me.

"Not coming in your pretty little mouth," I say as she scowls up at me. "Not this time."

And to my utter surprise and joy, she doesn't immediately lie down on her back.

No, my girl gets on all fours and shows me her glorious ass.

I'm in love.

I quickly protect us both, and with a light swat on one perfect cheek, I slide inside of her, and we both groan in ecstasy.

"Ah, shit," I moan. With both hands on her hips, I start to move, and Sophie leans into the bed, the covers fisted in her hands, as she pushes back on me in a perfect rhythm. It grows faster, harder, and I have to press one hand over the small of her back as I watch myself slide in and out as that little piece of skin moves in and out with me, and I know that I won't last much longer.

Sophie cries out and reaches down, pressing her fingers to her clit, and as she begins to convulse, so do I. I push in once more and come *hard.*

And when we've caught our breath, I leave the bed to discard the condom and get a warm, wet cloth for Sophie.

I clean her up myself as she lies there, completely unabashedly, and watches me.

"That was fun," she decides.

"Just fun?"

I toss the cloth aside and pull her under the covers with me. I don't give a flying fuck that it's the middle of the day.

"A *lot* of fun. And I think it's safe to say that the hangover is gone. It's amazing what approximately four orgasms will do for you."

I grin and kiss the tip of her nose. "Four? I only counted three."

"There were four. I came while I was going down on you."

I stare at her for a full five seconds, and then I can't help but laugh.

"Wow. That's hot as hell."

"So, I guess this means that we're getting married."

I pause, but the idea doesn't actually fill me with dread the way that it usually would. But before I can respond, she busts up laughing.

"I'm kidding. I was going to play the whole, *we had sex, so now we have to get married* routine, just for fun, but I couldn't pull it off."

I sigh and kiss her forehead. "So, you're *not* going to make an honest man out of me?"

She just giggles again and wraps her arm around my belly. "I like your sense of humor. I mean, your lovely abs are great, and I love how strong you are because you just toss me around like I weigh *nothing*, but the sense of humor is the sexiest part about you."

"Really?"

"Yeah. It's hot that you don't take yourself too seriously all the time. Just with sex, it seems. And I know that I'm babbling now, and probably saying way too much, but I have to just tell you that the whole assertive alpha male thing you have going on when it comes to sex is just...wow."

"I have that going on?"

She raises a head and stares at me. "You don't know it?"

"I don't think it's ever really occurred to me. I told you before, I just am who I am, sweetheart."

"And that's why it's hot."

IT'S BEEN A WEEK. One week of going about our lives, working, working *out, both* together and separately, and spending all of our spare time together.

One week of the best sex of my fucking life.

I can hear Sophie in her shower, talking to herself. It seems she does that a lot, whether she's in the shower, cooking, working out, you name it. She even talks in her sleep, which I find completely adorable.

It seems that everything she does is adorable.

I can't get enough of her.

And thankfully, it doesn't seem that she's sick of me yet, either.

I walk into her closet and pull on the clothes that

I've stashed there. It's only been one week, but we've each thrown a few necessities, including a change of clothes, in the other's home. It just makes sense because we never know for sure where we're going to end up for the night.

And she doesn't know it yet, but I'll eventually get her to move in with me.

Yes, it's fast, but I don't give a rat's ass. I'm completely smitten with her, and I want her with me all the time.

But for now, this works for us.

Sophie walks into the closet wearing her pink robe, and her hair is up in a matching pink towel.

"Hi there." I move in on her and open the sash of her robe, letting my hands glide around to cup her bare ass. "Let's go back to bed."

"I can't." She laughs and bites my chin, then brushes her naked breasts against me. "As much as I'd love to, I have to get ready for work. And you do, too."

"Yeah, yeah." I sigh and step back as she starts to pull on clothes. It looks like today's outfit is a pair of purple leggings, a white T-shirt, and a black jacket thing. "You must be filming today."

"We are. What are you up to?"

"I have to meet with my agent to go over the contract I've been offered, and then I'll work out with some of the guys. I need to go through some throwing exercises and start getting my shoulder back in the game."

"You've been offered a contract? From Seattle?"

"Yeah. I don't know the specifics yet, so keep your fingers crossed that it doesn't suck."

"It's not going to suck." She finishes tying an Air Jordan, then crosses to me and cups my face in her hands, kissing me. "It's going to be *awesome.* Only positive vibes, Ike."

I grin down at her. "You're a very good motivational coach."

"I know." She smiles back at me, then walks into the bedroom where her makeup station is. "Hey, I want to ask you something. How would you feel about attending my cousin's wedding with me? Liv and Vaughn are getting married in two weeks, and I want you to be my date."

I raise an eyebrow. "You do?"

"Yeah. You'll look fabulous on my arm. And you know Uncle Will and Aunt Meg. But you'll have to meet my dad there, too. Maybe we should do dinner with my parents beforehand so they can meet you when it's not at a big family event."

"I'm happy to go anywhere with you and meet whomever you want. No problem."

"Awesome, that was easy. Oh, and you'll need a tux."

"I happen to have one. Have you had coffee?"

"Not yet."

"I'll make you some."

"You're a lifesaver."

I wink and head out to the kitchen. I've just pulled

two mugs out of the cabinet when the front door opens, and I turn to find a woman, maybe in her mid-twenties, sputtering.

"Did I walk into the wrong condo?"

"I don't know. Which one were you hoping for?"

She looks back at the door, then at me. "Uh, Sophie's. This is right. Right?"

"This is Sophie's place," I confirm. "And you must be Becs. Coffee?"

"Uh, sure. Okay, yeah. Just black." She walks to the kitchen island and sets a bag on a stool. "Wait. Aren't you Ike Harrison?"

I grin at her. "I am. Nice to meet you."

She shakes my hand. When Sophie comes walking into the room, she just shifts her gaze back and forth between us until a Cheshire cat smile spreads over her pretty face.

"Holy. Shitballs."

"Hi, Becs." Sophie takes her mug from me and sips. "You're early."

"And it's a damn good thing because you haven't told me about this little tidbit of juicy information. How long have you been doing the hot football player?"

"You think I'm hot?" I lean on the counter and smile.

"Don't encourage him," Sophie says with a sigh but nudges me with her hip. "And we've been dating for just over a week."

"A week." Becs props her hands on her hips. "A *week*. And you haven't told me?"

"I apologize for not sending out the memo." Sophie's voice is dry, and it makes me laugh. She says that my sense of humor is hot, but it's one of the things I'm attracted to in her, as well. She can make me laugh like no one else.

It's just plain awesome and makes hanging out with her a blast.

"Are you staying?" Becs asks me.

"No, I'm on my way out. Have a good day, ladies." I pull Sophie against me, cup her face in one hand, and kiss her the way I have every time I've left her over the past week. And when I pull away, I can feel Becs staring a hole through us. "See you later, beautiful."

"See you."

I wink at Becs as I walk by, and then I'm out the door.

I'm anxious to meet up with Bill, my agent. I've been working with him since I was just out of college, and I trust him implicitly. I know that he'll get me the best deal possible.

Because I'm already in downtown Seattle, the drive to Bill's hotel isn't far. I was surprised that he wanted to come to town to discuss the contract, rather than go over things remotely.

It can't be good if he wants to do this in person.

I leave my truck with the valet and ride the elevator

up to Bill's room. When he opens the door, his face looks grim.

"Okay, I'm here. Give me the bad fucking news."

"Come on in, Ike. It's good to see you."

I walk into the suite and sit on the couch where Bill already has papers spread out on the coffee table.

"It's not as bad as you think," he continues.

"If it was awesome, you wouldn't want me to be here in person."

"That's not necessarily true. I do think that there are some things you and I are going to need to go over in a meeting with the team management because there are a couple of clauses that we absolutely won't agree to under any circumstances."

"Like what?"

He sits across from me and picks up a flagged piece of paper.

"Let me just read it to you. *Isaiah Harrison will not date or have any relationship, personal or professional, with anyone in Will Montgomery's family. Any breach of this agreement can lead to disciplinary action up to and including termination without the possibility of compensation for the remainder of his contract.*"

"I won't sign that bullshit."

"Absolutely not," he agrees. "I will say that they're offering you a nice amount of money. It's for ten years, at four hundred million dollars."

I blink and then clear my throat. "Holy shit."

"I think they can do better," he continues. "With

your talent, I think we can get that up another fifty million over the ten years, and we'll ask for that in negotiations. This isn't unprecedented, but it's significant, and I'm so proud of you, Ike."

I can't get past the amount of money.

"Ike? Are you not satisfied with the amount?"

"Uh, yeah. I'm happy with the amount. I'm not okay with that clause. If they won't take that out, there's no deal. I know I can get on with another team in a heartbeat."

"Without question," Bill agrees. "And I'm with you. They can't dictate your personal life like that. They're taking it too far. I know that Florence has had some personal troubles with the Montgomery family lately, but not even she has the authority to do this. I'll set up a meeting for this week."

"Okay, great. Thank you, Bill. I'm kind of surprised that you came all the way from LA for this."

"There's more." He smiles now, and I can tell that the hard part is over. "You've had several offers for endorsement opportunities. One is with a national insurance company, another is a sports drink, and yet another for a shoe."

"A shoe. Someone wants to give me my own *shoe?*"

This can't be real. I have to be dreaming.

"They do. There are a few other smaller ones, but the three I just mentioned would be an additional ten million per year combined."

All I can do is stare at Bill and feel so much gratitude for the man.

"So, you're saying that, within just a few weeks, I could be making upwards of fifty million a *year*?"

"That's what I'm saying. And that's on the low end."

"Well, damn."

"Congratulations, Ike. You're officially my top-grossing client."

Once I'm back in my truck, I sit and stare at the steering wheel for about five minutes, soaking it all in. That's a *lot* of money. That's life-changing money.

Not that it wasn't before, but this is a whole new level of wealth that I've never even dreamed of.

And if I'm not careful, my father will siphon away every fucking penny from me once this becomes public.

So, my first call is to Will Montgomery.

"Hey, Ike. Megan and I were just talking about you. What's up?"

"I know this is kind of weird, but are you busy? Like, can I come by and talk to you?"

"I'm actually not busy right now. We're home. Come on by."

"Thanks. I'm leaving downtown now, so it'll be about fifteen minutes or so."

"No rush. We'll see you soon."

I need advice, and Will's the only guy I know well who's been in this kind of position before.

I make my way through town and to Will's house.

The gate automatically opens because he's expecting me, and when I park in the circular driveway, I see the front door open, and Will steps outside.

"Sorry for the short notice," I say as I jog up his steps and shake his hand.

"Don't be. You're not interrupting anything." He takes in my face and nods. "Let's go to the office. Babe," he calls out, "we'll be in my office."

"Okay!" I hear Meg call back. "Hi, Ike!"

"Hi, Meg," I reply as I follow Will down a long hallway and into an office at the end of it. Will closes the door behind us, and rather than sitting behind his desk, he gestures to a chair in the corner, and he sits across from me on a facing sofa.

His trophies line the walls. Photos of Will with teammates, friends, and coaches. There's even a photo of the entire Montgomery family, all smiles, at one of the championship games that Will played in.

Sophie, no more than fifteen, is grinning at the camera.

"I like your office," I say at last.

"It's where I come to think when the girls get a little too loud."

I nod and shift in the seat.

"Okay, you're making *me* nervous. What's going on, Ike?"

"My agent is in town. My contract came in."

He raises a brow. "And?"

I outline everything for him, and when I'm done, he

whistles through his teeth. "That's a *damn* good contract. Jesus, congratulations, man."

"Thanks. There's one thing, though, and it's the reason Bill's in town. There's a clause I won't sign."

"For that amount of money? What is it?"

I have to stand and pace to the windows. "Florence had it written in that I'm not allowed to have any sort of relationship with you or any member of your family. A photo of Sophie and me leaked, and it pissed her off."

"Fuck her," he mutters, and I turn to look at him.

"Oh, yeah, fuck her sideways. I won't sign it. I'm in too deep with Soph, and even if I wasn't, it's the principle of it, you know?"

He narrows his eyes. "Yeah, I get it. Your lawyers can make her take it out, and she knows it. She's just throwing a fit in the only way she can."

I nod and lick my lips. "That's what Bill said, too. I made it clear that if she doubles down, I'll leave the team and go elsewhere, but Bill doesn't think it'll come to that."

"I'd be shocked if it did," he agrees.

I take a deep breath, lick my lips again, and sit back in the chair.

"What else is on your mind?"

"It's a lot of money," I say at last. "I need to keep my dad's fingers out of it. I'm *not* okay with sending home every dime I don't need. I can't keep doing it. Like you said, I need to be smart for when football is done, and I guess it's also the principle of it. I've asked around. No one else does for their families what I do for mine. Most everyone does *some*, but not like this."

"Thank Christ you saw the light," Will mutters and presses his fingers into his eyes. "Your father has no right to demand that much money from you. It sounds like you've set him up to be financially independent already."

"I thought I had, but the last time I spoke with him, he was pissed because I wasn't sending more money, and he said he has bills to pay. Will, I paid off everything. If he has bills, it's because he's being stupid."

"That's not on you," Will says, his voice hard as stone. "That's on *him.* Does he have access to any of your accounts?"

"No. He wanted it, but I put my foot down there. He only gets money that I transfer to him."

"Good. If you want my advice, I'm going to give it to you."

"That's why I'm here," I reply, keeping my eyes level with his.

"If I were in your shoes, I wouldn't give him another dime. I'd make sure my mom was okay, but when it came to Dad, no way. I would probably still send them on vacation once a year, or if there's a milestone anniversary or birthday, I'd give them a big gift, like a car or a boat or something. You said you've paid off their house?"

I nod in confirmation.

"Yeah, that's all I'd do. Your dad is going to try to make you feel like a complete asshole for this."

"Oh, I already know what's coming. I'm not afraid of confrontation until it comes to my dad. And then I'll do whatever it takes to make him happy. To make him proud. Because when he's *not* happy, the whole family suffers for it."

"You don't live under his roof," Will reminds me. "And if this means that you become estranged, well, that's on him. Not you. You've been more than generous. I have a whole team of financial advisors that I'm going to introduce you to right away. I want you to be prepared the minute that first check comes in. And, if it makes you feel better, let them be the fall guys. Tell your dad that it's not in your hands anymore."

"No, fuck that." I shake my head adamantly. "It's past time I stand up to him. I appreciate the help. I don't even know the first step of dealing with that much money."

"Which is why I'm putting you in touch with my team. They're not cheap, but they'll make you back everything you spend with them. They can put you on a budget if you need one. And they're always a phone call away if you have questions, need money transferred, or whatever you need. Want a house in Tuscany? It's yours with just a phone call."

"Fucking hell."

I let my head fall back and rest it on the wall.

"Now, let's talk about my niece."

I lift my head again so I can give him another steady look. "Okay."

"What's going on there?"

"I don't think you want me to answer that."

Will bares his teeth, and I smirk.

"We're happy. She's funny as hell and so damn smart. Even has me drinking that green shit. And Jesus, is she ever beautiful. She just *glows*, and I know that sounds mushy and stupid, but it's true."

"Not stupid," Will says, his voice softer now. "Mushy as hell, but not stupid."

"We're doing well. She invited me to Olivia and Vaughn's wedding."

"Wow, it *is* going well, then. Soph doesn't bring men around the family."

"Really?"

He nods, and I take a deep breath.

"I plan to be with her for a long time. Whether Florence likes it or not."

"She won't like it. She'll hate it even more that there's nothing she can do about it."

"I hope that's the case because I don't want to leave Seattle, Will. I love this team. The coach is the best I've ever had, and my teammates are awesome. We're *winning*. And now that I have Sophie, I would happily play out my entire career here."

"Let Bill and the attorneys deal with Florence. Celebrate that contract. And get everything set up financially with the advisors before it goes public so your dad can't try to take what he seems to think is his cut."

I nod. "Yeah. Yeah, that's the plan."

"Congratulations, Ike. You've earned this, you know."

I grin, and for the first time since I left Bill's room, I let myself get excited. "I did. And I'll keep earning it."

"And that's why you deserve it."

CHAPTER 9

SOPHIE

"We've filmed three videos," Becs says and scoops her long, dark hair into a high messy bun. "Taken about two hundred photos, made a shopping list, and I even helped you pick out your outfit for Olivia's bachelorette party on Friday night."

"I'm *so* excited about that," I reply with a nod. "Did I tell you that we're going dancing downtown? I haven't been dancing in *ages*."

"Will you have security?" Becs asks, her brows lowering in concern.

"A couple of the brothers are driving us," I reply with a shrug. "And I'm sure Vaughn will have security follow us, knowing him."

"Wait. You're getting me off-topic. We did all this work today," she continues as she helps me clean up some of the mess from cooking, "and not *one time* did you tell me about Ike and how good he is in bed."

"I'm not telling you that," I reply at last and turn to frown at my friend. "He's...*different*. Not just a fling. And I think it's disrespectful to talk about our sex life with anyone. Not because I don't trust and love you, but because I want to keep our intimacy between the two of us."

She blinks at me, and then a smile spreads over her pretty face. "You're in love."

"Stop it." I shake my head and go back to loading the dishwasher. "I'm just not a college kid anymore who thinks it's funny to trade sex stories, that's all. If I found out he was spilling details to his football buddies, I'd be hella pissed off."

She tips her head from side to side, thinking it over. "Okay, I can see that. Just tell me *one* thing."

"No."

"Is it good?" she asks, relentlessly. "Like, on a scale of one to ten?"

I stare down at the glass mixing bowl in my hands and bite my lip before looking back up at Becs. "There's not a number high enough, Becs."

"Holy. Shit." She pretends to faint against the kitchen island dramatically and then busts up with giggles. "It's about damn time you had a hot man rock your world."

"Oh, he's rocking it all right. He's doing a good job of that."

We laugh again and then finish loading the dishwasher and starting it before packing up some leftovers for her to take home.

"I'll have videos edited and ready for you to post to social media by Friday," she promises. "Photos by tomorrow morning."

"I appreciate it." I lean in to kiss her cheek. "Thanks for being happy for me and not a jealous bitch."

"I mean, I *can* be a jealous bitch on occasion," she replies and wrinkles her nose. "But not over this. You deserve to be happy, whether that's with a hot quarterback or by yourself. Just be happy, Soph."

"I am." I walk her to the door. "I'm really happy right now."

"Good. Okay, have a good one, and I'll see you in a few days."

"See you."

I close the door behind her and grab a protein drink on the way to my office so I can fire up the computer and get to work answering emails, posting today's content on social media, and engaging with people in the comments.

One of the reasons I've grown my business the way I have is because I'm accessible to people. I *want* to help them in any way I can.

When I've finished with the engagement part of my day, I open another browser and begin looking into merchandise.

There are a few catchphrases that I have, including,

Love yourself as you are right now, and *Beautiful isn't a size.*

Followers have asked me for more than a year to put these on shirts, mugs, bags, you name it, but I had to have them trademarked first. And now that I've finished that crazy process, we can start putting out the merchandise.

I wonder if one, or both, of my teenage cousins would like a part-time job to help with this. I'll have to make a note to ask them.

I've just turned off the computer and am staring out the window when my phone rings.

Not a text, a *call.*

That's when I know something is serious.

I frown at Olivia's name and answer. "Hey, you."

I hear her sniffle and then, "I'm not marrying Vaughn."

Standing, I hurry through the condo to put on shoes and grab my purse. "What? Why? Are you hurt?"

"I'm *so fucking mad.*"

"Okay. I've got you. Where are you right now?"

"At work." More sniffles. "And I'm locked in my office because I can't let anyone see me like this. Stella's on her way, but she's in Olympia on a job, and that's really far."

"I'll be there in ten minutes," I promise her, trying to decide if I should walk or drive. Depending on traffic, speed-walking might be faster.

"Okay," she says and sniffs again. "I'll let them know you're coming."

"Ten minutes," I say again and hang up, deciding to drive. And for today, I'm in luck because traffic doesn't suck, and I'm able to get to the Williams Productions building in less than six minutes.

I park in what Uncle Luke has designated as family parking and hurry into the building.

Thankfully, security knows me and buzzes me right through.

When I make it to Olivia's office, I open the door, close it behind me, and hurry over to where she's curled up at the end of a sofa that looks out to the city.

Liv is a gorgeous woman, but right now, her pretty green eyes are puffy from crying, and her face is blotchy, and she just looks miserable.

"Oh, honey." I pull her to me and hold her tight as a whole new crying jag starts. "Let it out. It's okay to let it all out."

"I'm so mad."

"I know. I cry when I'm mad, too." I lean over and grab the box of tissues, offering her one. "When you can breathe again, you can tell me what happened."

"So stupid," she manages to get out through the sobs. "So fucking stupid."

"They usually are," I reply, and she lets out a half laugh through the tears, which gives me hope. For a while, we sit like this, with me patiently rubbing her back as she runs out of energy for tears.

Finally, Liv sits up, grabs a few tissues, and blows her nose before sighing and looking at me with angry eyes.

"What did he do?"

"He refuses to invite his parents to the wedding." She swipes at her nose and stands to pace her office. "I mean, who even *does* that? I understand that they're not super close. There's a lot of baggage there, but they're his parents. His *parents.*"

She flings her arms over her head and starts pacing even faster.

"Like, when we have kids, and if it's twenty-five years from now and our son is getting married, would Vaughn be perfectly fine if we're not invited to the freaking ceremony? If we're not involved in *any* of it? I would be devastated!"

"Okay, first of all, you're not pregnant. Wait, you're not pregnant, are you?"

"No." She stares at me like I've lost my mind.

"Just clarifying. Do you need me to help you with solutions, or do you need me to hate him?"

And just like that, my strong, brave, wonderful cousin deflates and just sits down on the floor.

"I guess I always pictured myself marrying someone who has the kind of family that *we* do, Soph."

"Oh, honey, no one has a family like ours." I blow out a breath and walk over to the small fridge she has in the corner, pull out two bottled waters, and take her one before cracking open my own. "I don't really understand how people can be estranged from their families, especially their parents, because we come from amazing people. We come from a family that, although a lot to handle, makes us kids a top priority. Puts their marriages first, even before *us*. That's what we were lucky enough to grow up in."

"Yeah, I know."

"But, Liv, not everyone else is so lucky. There are so many people out there with kids who had no business procreating in the first place. Or maybe they're sick. Or they just don't put their kids very high on their priority list. I don't know much about Vaughn's family, just what I've seen from the documentary and in the things I've read, but his celebrity family is the complete opposite of yours. Uncle Luke protected you guys from so much. Vaughn's family is a true show business family."

"I'm being unreasonable."

"I think you just picture your wedding a certain way, with all the parents happy and excited for you. Have you ever thought that maybe Vaughn's parents don't want to be there, and he isn't willing to put himself in a situation where he'll be rejected? Especially when it comes to something this important to him?"

Liv bites her lip, and more tears fill her eyes. "I'm such a selfish bitch."

"Okay, stop it." I shake my head at her. "You're under a *lot* of stress, Liv. I don't know how anyone throws together a wedding of this size in a month.

There are so many details, and you haven't reached out to any of us for help."

"I feel bad asking for help," she admits. "I'm the one who insisted on making it fast, mostly because the press are a bunch of assholes, and I refuse to let them ruin this for us. That doesn't mean I should be putting everyone else out. Besides, Aunt Alecia has been a huge help at the vineyard."

"I'm sure she's in her element," I agree. Our aunt Alecia was the family event planner long before she married our uncle Dominic. "What else do you need help with? We're only two weeks out now."

"Well, first, I should tell Vaughn that I'm *not* breaking up with him."

I stare at her and then reach over and poke her in the arm.

"Ouch."

"You *broke up* with Vaughn?"

"I was really upset."

"Look, I'm no relationship expert, but you can't threaten to cut and run every time you get upset. That's annoying as fuck and not fair."

"It's the first and only time it's happened." She reaches for her phone and taps the screen. When Vaughn answers, she frowns. "Are you *driving*?"

"I'm almost to your office," he says. I can hear the tension in his voice. Poor guy. "Don't move a muscle. I'll be there in two minutes."

Before Liv can reply, he hangs up.

"So, I guess we're moving forward with the bachelorette party on Friday," I say with a grin. "Which is good because we're going to dance our asses off, drink like it's free, and have the time of our lives. You need to let loose."

"Oh, I can't get drunk. I have too much to do."

"Bullshit." I grin at her as I hear footsteps running down the hallway. "Your knight in shining armor is here."

The door bursts open, and a feral-looking Vaughn scans the room. Good God, the man is beautiful. There's a reason why he's the hottest man in Hollywood. And when he's like this? Well, it's enough to make my ovaries sit up and do the happy dance.

His eyes stop scanning when he gets to Olivia.

"The wedding is absolutely *not* off," he says as he stalks to her, pulls her to her feet, and proceeds to kiss the hell out of her.

I stand and reach for my purse, but neither of them is paying any attention to me.

"Okay, well, I'm glad I could help. I hope you have a great day."

No reaction. Just lots of sloppy kisses.

"Okay, bye."

I wave and walk out the door, then close it behind me so they have privacy. I hit the button for the elevator, and the doors open, surprising me when I find Stella staring back at me.

"Crisis averted."

"Thank God." She presses her hand to her chest and leans back on the wall of the elevator. "I'll go see if she needs anything."

"She doesn't." I make her stay in the elevator with me and grin. "Vaughn just arrived, and they're making out pretty hardcore. Clothes might be gone by now."

"Ew." Stella scrunches up her nose. "I guess I didn't have to speed all the way from Olympia to get here. Liv's been a wreck lately."

"Yeah, that's what I gathered. The days of her doing everything by herself, aside from what Aunt Alecia has been able to do, are over. We'll help her."

"We'll make her let us help," Stella agrees with a firm nod. "Every time I ask, she just blows me off. No more."

"She seems to think she can't get drunk Friday night."

Stella smirks. "Challenge accepted."

"That's what I thought. Well, now that your day has been interrupted, what are your plans?"

"You know, I think I'll go to my own fiancé's office and see if I can steal him away for a while. Get some naked time in of my own."

"I can't believe you're engaged, too. Have you set a date?"

"Nah, probably sometime next year. I want to enjoy this time, you know? Besides, Liv's getting married next month, and Josie recently eloped. Maddie will probably end up engaged to Dylan before long."

"I like him," I add with a smile as we walk out into the spring sunshine. "I can't believe she met him on an airplane on the way to Iceland, which is something out of a Hallmark movie."

"I do, too. I guess the point is, it's a lot for the family right now, and I'm not really in a hurry. Maybe we'll aim for the fall... when the trees are turning."

"That would be beautiful."

Stella takes a deep breath, tips her face up to the sunshine, and then smiles at me.

"Yeah, it would, wouldn't it? I'll talk to Gray about it."

"Speaking of liking guys, Stel, I really like your Gray. He suits you. I've never seen you so confident or just so content. And it makes me so happy for you."

"Thanks. I *am* happy. Sometimes I wonder if things are too good, you know? How are things with Ike?"

The smile on my face must tell her everything she needs to know because she cackles and then wraps her arms around me in a big hug.

"Hell yes, girl. I'm so damn excited for you. He's hot as can be, and he seems so *nice.*"

"He's all of that. And he's just really...great. I'm just waiting for the other shoe to drop. Like, things are just too good."

"Don't be a Debbie Downer," she says. "And I'll try to follow the same advice. What's that you always say? Positive vibes only?"

"I didn't know that you watched my stuff."

Stella digs her keys out of her bag. "We all do, babe. We're fucking proud of you. Now, go find your football player for some naked time of your own."

"Good idea. See you Friday."

"Wear something you don't mind ruining," she suggests. "I have a feeling it's going to get out of control."

"Promises, promises."

Stella laughs and waves as she walks away.

Rather than drive home, I call Ike.

"Hey, beautiful."

"Hi yourself. Are you all finished with your meetings?"

"Actually, I am. What are you up to?"

"I was thinking about going home, taking a shower, and then waiting in my bed, naked, for you to get there."

There's the slightest pause. "Number one, I'm glad you're not on speakerphone. Number two, you won't be waiting long."

"Great."

I hang up, and, with a bounce in my step, I hurry home.

I'VE JUST FINISHED SHAVING my legs when the door to my shower opens, and a very naked Ike steps inside.

Speaking of beautiful men... Ike's body looks like

it's been sculpted out of marble. He's just perfect. All muscled and smooth and *mine.*

"I didn't even get to climb in bed," I say before I'm pinned to the cold tile wall and Ike's lips are on mine, feasting.

That's the only way I can describe it. Every time we're together, he's so intent on me, so ravenous that it's as though he's *feasting* on me.

And I freaking love it. I can't get enough of him, either.

Ike boosts me up, and as I wrap my legs around his waist, he slides right inside of me, making me gasp in delight.

"Been thinking about you all day," he growls against my neck. "And how fucking good you feel."

I always enjoy being with this man, but *this* is my favorite side of him. The possessive, intense side.

With his eyes pinned to mine, he drives himself hard, in and out, chasing the orgasm until it makes its way through both of us, leaving us gasping for breath.

Ike slides out of me and gently sets me down on my feet, and then, with the gentlest hands, he cleans us up, turns off the hot water, and proceeds to dry me himself.

"You're dripping," I say as he rubs my skin with the terry cloth.

"You first," he says. "Always."

"Aren't you cold?"

"After that? Hell no." He nibbles on my lips, and once I'm dry, he uses the same towel on himself.

"I'm gonna go get dressed."

"No."

I turn at his stern voice, already turned on again. "Excuse me?"

"You promised me naked bed time." He tosses the towel aside, takes my hand, and leads me to the bedroom. "We're not done, sweetheart."

"Well, okay then."

I happily climb into my bed and smile at him.

"What brought this on, anyway?" he asks.

"Stella suggested it."

His brows furrow in surprise. "I wasn't expecting that answer, but I knew I liked her."

I laugh and reach for him. "It's a long story."

"You can tell me when we're done. Much, much later."

"Deal."

CHAPTER 10

IKE

"I'm not excited about this meeting." I lean on my countertop and watch Sophie stuff a bunch of spinach into the smoothie she's making in the new blender she bought for my kitchen.

God, I love having her in my house. I don't even mind the green smoothies anymore.

"I know you're not. But let your agent and the attorney handle it. They're the experts."

"I just want to play football," I say and rub my hands over my face. "The details annoy the shit out of me."

"The details of any job are annoying," she reminds me and passes me a glass of the smoothie. "But we have to deal with them so we can do the part we enjoy. You'll get through this today, and when it's finished, you're good to go for a while."

"That's the goal," I reply and tap my glass to hers.

When I told Sophie that I'd been offered the

contract the other day, she didn't ask me how much it was for. The only thing she wanted to know was if I was happy with the offer and if I'd be staying here.

Most women would want the details. Hell, I can't blame anyone for being curious.

"You didn't ask me how much they offered me."

"That's none of my business," she replies and sips her drink before dismantling the blender and rinsing it.

"The rest of the world would disagree. If I sign today, ESPN will be reporting about it tonight, down to every detail."

"See, I think that's bullshit. I know that people are curious, especially when it comes to the wealthy. They want to know how much actors are paid to appear in films, and how much athletes make on their contracts. Hell, they even want to know how much *I* make from my stuff. And I do well, but I'm not on the elite tier of things. I just think it's stupid. I don't walk around town meeting people and breaking the ice with, *so, what did you bring in last year?*"

"No." I laugh and drain the glass, then set it in the dishwasher. "I guess the curiosity factor increases with the net worth, so to speak."

I blow out a breath. I haven't yet confided in Sophie about my father. Not because I don't want her to know, but because I just don't want to talk about him. But I'd be an ass if I didn't give her a heads-up.

"You should know that my family will cause some trouble."

She turns to me now, her face lined with concern. "In what way?"

"Well, specifically, my father will have his hand out, as usual. I don't want to burden you with the details, but my dad's a leech. And when ESPN reports on the compensation amount of this contract, he'll expect the bulk of it to go to him."

"What in the actual fuck?"

I can't help but grin. "Exactly. Thanks to Will, I already have a team of people on standby to help me with things, and my dad won't be able to touch any of the money, but that will only piss him off more. I'll be able to handle it, but I just thought you should know because... well, because you matter to me."

Sophie crosses to me and frames my face in her hands. "You've taken care of yourself? Protected yourself?"

"Yeah. I have." I take one of her hands in mine and kiss her palm. "But it could get dramatic for a minute."

"Don't worry about me." She wraps her arms around me and hugs me tight, and I've never had the urge to tell a woman that I love her more than I do right now. Her support is everything. "Get through the meeting, then deal with the next thing. One step at a time, Ike."

"You're right." I kiss the top of her head. "Thanks."

"So, I guess it's a lot of money?" She frowns up at me. She doesn't look hungry or excited or calculating.

She still looks concerned.

"Yeah. It's a shit ton of money."

"Good for you. When it's all said and done, we're going to celebrate that."

"I'm in." I wink down at her, kiss her lips softly, and then step away. "I'd better go. We're meeting over at headquarters in thirty."

"You've got this. I don't know what it is that you're negotiating, but you've totally got this."

I kiss her again, then grab my keys and wallet and head out to my truck parked down the driveway.

I didn't tell Sophie that *she* is the main point that I'm negotiating.

The ironic thing is that a month ago, this wouldn't even be a thing. I didn't know her then, and Florence would have no reason to include Sophie in the contract. I likely would have signed by now, and it would be a done deal.

The timing of things is just crazy.

But, I *did* meet Sophie, and I'm well on my way to falling in love with her. I'm not giving her up for Florence or anyone else.

I pull into my parking space at the practice facility. The headquarters offices are in the adjoining building, and when I walk inside, I see that Bill is waiting for me in the lobby.

"You look great," he says, as if surprised, and I look down at my black slacks and blue shirt.

"I almost wore a tie, but I thought that might be overkill."

Bill laughs and smooths his hand down his own tie. I've never seen the man outside of a suit, even in a casual setting.

I kind of like that about him. He's professional.

"Like I said yesterday on the phone," I begin, getting right to the chase, "if she won't back down, I'm out."

"I have two calls from other teams," he says softly, almost whispering into my ear, which is probably smart. There are ears everywhere. "San Francisco and Denver would match the terms."

I narrow my eyes. "Good to know."

"Hello, gentlemen."

We turn at the voice behind us. Brandon Lily is Florence's assistant. For now. She goes through assistants like she does underwear.

"Hi, Brandon," I say.

"They're ready for you," Brandon replies and gestures for us to follow him.

The first thing I notice is the huge table in the middle of the conference room. Florence is sitting at the head of the table, her hair dyed a fiery red, and she's dressed in a black suit. She's flanked by several men, also in black suits, whom I assume are her attorneys.

My attorney is already here, and Bill and I take our seats next to him.

For the next fifteen minutes, I sit quietly and listen to the attorneys go back and forth on little nitpicky things, like the pay schedule.

And when they get to the Montgomery clause, I glance up to see Florence staring holes into me.

She likes to be intimidating. I know she can be a ruthless bitch. She didn't purchase this football team because of her love of the game. No, she inherited it.

And she loves the power she has because of it.

But I bet she wouldn't know a touchdown from a kick in the ass.

"There's no cause for this clause in the contract," my attorney, Richard, begins. "My client is an employee, not a slave. The team can't dictate who he's friends with or with whom he has a romantic relationship."

"Yes, I can," Florence says, not taking her eyes off me. She looks good and pissed. "The Montgomery family has declared war on this team, and I will not have my players fraternizing with them."

"Uh, Will is still on as an advisor."

Her eyes narrow at my comment. "That's none of your business."

I sit back and blow out a breath.

"Ike won't sign the contract with this clause in it," Bill says. "Not under any circumstances."

"Then I suppose he can't play for me."

She's staring me down, playing a ridiculous game of chicken. So, I stand and turn to Bill, who's still sitting.

"Call San Francisco. I'll lead *them* to a championship next year."

I turn to leave, and Florence says with a tight voice, "Wait."

I look back at her and raise an eyebrow, not saying a word.

"You can't just toss out empty threats of going to another team." Her lips press together, making them almost disappear.

"It's not empty. I have other offers. I know that I can lead our team through the playoffs next season, just like we did this season. We were so close to winning the championship, I could smell it. I can't guarantee that, of course, but we have a talented lineup, and I know we can be successful. I want to stay *here.* But I won't sign a contract that has anything to do with the Montgomerys in it. If you won't waver on that, we don't have anything else to discuss, and I thank you for four great years here."

One of her attorneys leans over and whispers in her ear. Florence blinks, sighs, and speaks through her teeth.

"Fine. I'll take it out. But I want it known right here and now that I do *not* like the idea of my star player having anything at all to do with a family that would like to see the ruin of our team."

"I'm sorry you feel that way all around, ma'am. I don't think they want to see the ruin of this team."

"You're wrong." And with that, she turns to the attorney who spoke in her ear. "Have the final draft drawn up, *now*, and let's sign and get it over with. I'll want the press here within thirty minutes for a statement."

"I don't—"

"I don't care what you *don't*," Florence interrupts. "Make it happen."

Laptops are opened, Brandon already has his phone in his hand as he scrambles out the door, and I simply turn to Bill.

"I need some air."

I walk out the doors and down the hall, then press the button for the elevator as Bill joins me. We don't say a word as we ride down to the ground level, and I walk out a side door where I know no one else is.

I take a deep breath and let it out slowly.

"I hate that she owns this team," I mutter.

"I know," he says. "She's never cared about her players. But she *does* own the team, and I'm glad her attorney was able to talk some sense into her."

"Did we really have other offers on the table, or did you tell me that to bolster my confidence so I'd stand my ground?"

He grins. "We have more than two others, Ike."

"Nice."

~

"I'M SO PROUD OF YOU," Sophie says as we drive through the city on our way to her parents' house for dinner. It was a last-minute arrangement, but one I didn't mind.

It'll keep my mind on something other than waiting for my old man to call once the sports channels start airing the news of the day, which should be just about any time.

"I'm happy that it all went well," I say and follow the GPS.

"I'm sorry that we're not celebrating by ourselves," Sophie adds and takes my hand in hers. "But Mom called and said that they'd love to have us for dinner, and I just said yes without really thinking about it."

"It's fine with me. Honest. We can celebrate anytime." I turn into the driveway and kill the engine, smiling over at her. "I might be a little nervous."

"Are you kidding? You play football for thousands of people. Millions, if you count the TV viewers."

"None of them are the father of the girl I'm dating. That's a whole different level of intimidating."

Sophie just laughs and opens her door.

"Wait." I jump out and hurry around to help her out of my truck, and before we get to the front door, it swings open, and Sophie's parents are waiting.

I recognize her mother from the bridal shower, and her dad looks a lot like Will.

"Mom, Dad, this is Ike."

"It's good to see you again," I say as Stacy offers me her hand, and then I turn to Isaac, who's watching me with blue eyes just like his daughter's. "Hello, sir."

"Isaac," he replies and shakes my hand. "Just call me Isaac. Come on in. I have some steaks on the grill. Help me with that, will you, Ike?"

"You bet." I follow the other man through the house and out the back door to a nice patio and backyard. "It's great back here."

"The kids loved it when they were little," Isaac says and opens the grill to check the steaks. "How do you like your meat?"

"Medium is great."

He nods and flips them over, then closes the lid.

"How did you meet my daughter?"

"I swept her off her feet." I grin, but he just stares at me, so I explain how I ran into her at the park and then again later that day at Will's. "I just kept running into her and couldn't get her off my mind. So, I asked her out."

"And now?"

I accept the beer he offers me and take a drink. I haven't had a beer in months, and it tastes good today.

"Now, I can't get enough of her. She's so damn smart. Gorgeous. Funny."

"Yeah." He opens the grill again. "She is all of that. And if you hurt her, I'll kill you."

"Will also already threatened that."

"I have several brothers who will help, who know

how to make it look like an accident, and no one will ever find the body."

He's not kidding, and we both know it.

"Understood."

My phone rings, and I glance down at it, see my father's name, and send him to voice mail.

And so it begins.

"So, you're from Oklahoma originally?" Isaac asks.

"I am. I prefer the Pacific Northwest. I like the weather, being close to the ocean, and pretty much everything."

"You like the *weather*?"

"I do. I don't mind the rain, and it's not bitter cold in the winter like what we get in Oklahoma. And no tornadoes."

"That's true." He pulls the steaks off the grill and puts them on a plate, then covers them just as my phone rings again. "These steaks have to rest."

I send my dad to voice mail.

Isaac eyes my phone. "Is that your father?"

"Yeah." I sip my beer.

"Maybe you should answer it."

There is no part of me that wants to take this call, especially in front of Sophie's dad.

"He can wait."

But my phone rings again, and I blow out a breath.

"Maybe there's an emergency," Isaac says.

There's no emergency.

But I answer anyway.

"Hey, Dad."

"Son! I just saw the news on ESPN. FOUR HUNDRED MILLION!! I'm so fucking proud of you. I guess I can get my truck now, after all."

"Look, Dad, now's not a good time."

"You go find some pussy to celebrate. Don't spend all my money, now. Call me tomorrow, yeah?"

"Right. Bye, Dad."

I hang up and feel like throwing my phone as hard as I can across the backyard.

"You heard that."

Isaac just nods. "Yeah, I heard."

"*That's* who I come from. And I'm not proud of it."

We're quiet for a moment, and then Isaac lays his hand on my shoulder. "You may come from him, but you're *not* him. I just met you, and I already know that, Ike."

"No, I'm not him. But I have to deal with him."

"I'm always around if you want to talk."

I look over at him. Sophie looks a lot like her dad and uncles. "Thanks. I think I've figured out how to handle it. Now I just have to do it."

"Fast and firm," he replies, then picks up the plate of steaks. "That's the best way. Be swift and be firm in your stance."

I nod and follow Isaac into the house. "You're right about that."

For the rest of the evening, we leave the call from

my dad and everything to do with him out of the conversation.

Stacy shows me baby pictures of Sophie, which makes Soph blush. And I just have a great time with them. They're genuine, don't give a shit about what I do for a living, and make me feel welcome.

On the way home, Sophie grins over at me.

"What?" I ask her.

"I knew they'd like you, but I think my mom wants to marry you."

"Too bad for me that she's already married." I wink at her, making her laugh.

"Thanks for being so nice to them. I love them a lot."

"I know you do. And you should. They're pretty awesome."

"You like them?" Her voice is full of hope, and I frown over at her.

"I mean, what's not to like? They're great."

She nods happily. "I think *you're* great."

I waggle my eyebrows at her. "Yeah? How great do you think I am?"

"I mean, you're totally getting laid tonight, so pretty damn fantastic."

"So, this is an all-day bachelorette party." I pull up to the spa in Bellevue that Sophie gave me directions to and turn to her, reaching out to cup her gorgeous face.

"Yep. We're getting glammed up here first, then we're getting dinner so we don't get drunk too quickly, and then we're totally getting drunk and dancing our asses off for several hours. Possibly all night. It's going to be freaking *awesome*."

I laugh and tuck her soft hair behind her ear.

"You know, it occurs to me that this is the second time I've had drinking on the agenda since I met you, but I do *not* usually drink this much. I promise."

"I'm not complaining." I lean over to kiss her. "Have a blast. Call me if you need a ride."

"Will do. Have a good evening." She gets out of the truck and calls out to someone. "Haley's here. See you later."

She slams the door and bounces away, clearly excited to spend the day with her girls.

Just as I take off from the spa, my phone rings with a number I don't recognize.

"Hello."

"Mr. Harrison, this is Monica with Oklahoma First Bank. I need to confirm some spending on an account that you co-own with Clark Harrison."

My stomach sinks into my knees. "Okay. What's up?"

"He just came in and tried to withdraw seventy-thousand dollars, but there aren't enough funds to cover that transaction. In fact, there are very few funds in the account at all, and he made a scene in the lobby."

I swear under my breath. "I'm sorry about that. You're right, there isn't enough money in the account for that kind of transaction, nor will there be."

"Understood."

"Monica, if I want to close that account, do I need to do it in person? And does Clark need to be with me?"

"He doesn't need to be with you, no. And we *can* close it remotely, but it's always easier to do so in person."

"I see. Thank you."

"Have a nice day."

I hang up and toss my phone onto the floorboard of the truck.

It looks like I'm headed home to make arrangements to go to Oklahoma.

CHAPTER 11

SOPHIE

"My toes have never been prettier." I lean over and admire Haley's toes, polished in red, and grin.

"They're gorgeous. Can you believe that your sister's getting married?"

"I can." Haley sips her soda water and leans back in the pedicure chair, soaking in the massage. "Liv's always been the grounded one, the maternal one. She was *made* for marriage and babies."

"And what about you?" I lift an eyebrow as Haley busts up laughing. "What, no marriage for you?"

"I'm only twenty-two. So, not for a while, anyway. I definitely haven't met any guys who would be worthy of walking down the aisle to."

"I think that's pretty normal for your age," Stella chimes in from a few chairs down. "I mean, not *always*, of course, but most guys aren't ready to settle down in their early twenties. Besides, you just finished school. There's no rush."

"There's no rush for any of us," Erin says and sighs in happiness when the esthetician lays a hot towel over her legs.

Some of us got pedicures. Others opted for manicures. Some chose facials.

This whole spa is crawling with us cousins, and it's so dang fun.

We invited the old ladies, as we call them, to join us, but they bowed out and said that we should just enjoy each other without worrying about them.

Not that they're ever a worry.

I was the eldest cousin for a little while until Maddie and Josie came into the family. I don't remember a time before them, since I was just a toddler when their mom fell in love with my uncle Caleb. The three of us, the oldest cousins, have seen all the babies after us come into the family and grow up. We've mentored them. Listened when they didn't want to talk to their mothers about boys or bullying or anything, really.

There are twelve female cousins. We outnumber the boys by more than two to one.

That's a lot of estrogen.

But we're more than cousins. I've always thought of us as siblings because we are so entrenched in each other's lives. We love like siblings. And we fight like them, too.

"I have an idea," Stella announces, sitting up in her chair with excitement.

"Tell us," I reply.

"What if we keep this as planned, and the dinner, too, but we've rented out the dance club for just us, so why don't we invite the guys to meet us there and dance with us?"

"Can't you stay away from Gray for just *one day?*" Liv asks Stella, looking fresh and relaxed after a facial.

"Come on, you guys know that I love dancing with you, but it's way more fun with boys there."

"Wait, you rented out the club?" I ask.

"Vaughn did." Liv shrugs her shoulder. "He didn't love the idea of all of us clubbing without security because I said that I wouldn't have a bunch of dudes watching my every move, so he just rented out the club for the night."

"So, now we don't get to flirt with anyone?" Chelsea says. "That's lame."

"We could go to a different club." I tap my finger to my chin, thinking it over.

"You're trying to get me divorced before I even get married," Liv says with a laugh. "I'm telling you, Vaughn fits in really well with all of our dads. His main priority is safety, given who we all are and how stupid the tabloids are."

"The men in our family don't want us to have any fun," Zoey says with a scowl. "Since I don't get to flirt with eligible men, and it's likely that my boy cousins will turn up tonight, I'm going to eat my weight in pasta at dinner."

"Same, girl," Lucy agrees.

"We don't have to invite the guys," Stella says. "It's really not that big of a deal. I just thought it would be fun."

"I think they were feeling left out," Josie says, surprising me.

"Really?"

"Yeah, I talked to Drew earlier, and he seemed a little down that the guys don't get to help us celebrate Liv tonight, since they're close to her, too."

"Okay, now I feel bad," Liv says. "Let's invite the men to dance with us. We keep dinner just for ourselves, and they can come be silly at the club. We just won't let Liam go streaking."

I snort at that idea. My little brother went streaking *one time*. Sure, there have been other times that he strips down and jumps in the pool.

He's always had a thing about being naked. Weirdo.

"I'll text Liam and Ike," I say, reaching for my phone. Everyone does the same to let their brothers and significant others know to meet us.

Not one of them turns us down.

"I'm kind of excited about this," I say as we walk outside to where the limos are waiting to take us to dinner. We're all glammed up and ready to hit the town.

~

DINNER WAS DELICIOUS, and most of us ate as much pasta and bread as our bellies could hold and still look good in our dresses.

Which, surprisingly, was a lot.

And when we walk up to the club, the first thing the bouncer says is, "Where are Abby and Emma?"

The two youngest cousins step forward, their eyes wide.

"This is a private party, so while I know they're underage, I'd love to include them," Olivia says to the brawny bouncer.

"That's fine, ma'am, but I have to mark their hands so the bartender knows not to serve them alcohol."

He pulls a black marker out of his coat and draws big X's on their hands.

"Not pretty but necessary. Y'all have fun tonight. I'm out here to make sure no one crashes your fun."

"Thank you."

We all high-five him as we walk inside. The music is already loud, the lights pulsing, and from what I can see, our guys are already here.

I scan through them and find Ike at the bar, sipping on ice water.

"I'm sorry! I thought we'd get here before you so that I could introduce you to everyone."

"No worries," he says with a smile and plants a kiss on my lips. "I introduced myself."

"We like him," Liam says with a nod. "It's all good."

Standing next to Ike, with our backs against the bar, we take it all in together.

"That's a lot of women," he says.

"There are a lot of us." I laugh and accept a lemon drop martini from the bartender. "I think I'll slowly introduce you to everyone as time goes on. It's a little less intimidating that way."

"I can live with that. You smell fucking fantastic."

I grin and lean my cheek on his shoulder. "Thanks. I love that spa."

"I'm going to get you a weekly standing appointment there."

I look up at him in surprise and then laugh. "I wouldn't say no to that. Oh! I love this song. Let's go shake it."

"Just to warn you, I'm not a great dancer."

"I don't care at all."

I take his hand and lead him onto the dance floor, where Liv and Vaughn are locked in an embrace, and Stella is making gagging faces at them.

"They're getting married next week," I remind her. "Let them be mushy."

"Fine, but after the wedding, no more mushy."

"Hey," Gray says with a frown. "I like mushy."

We're all on the floor, jumping and moving and being goofy. Sometimes, we take breaks to get a drink or use the restroom, but for the most part, all of us are just dancing the night away.

And when the DJ plays a slow song, Ike pulls me into his arms to sway on the floor. I've never been so comfortable in my life. He says he can't dance, but he's wrong. He moves his big body incredibly well.

It's damn hot.

But I've noticed all evening that there's something in his eyes that doesn't look happy. Not at all. He's doing a great job of covering it up, but I know something is still bothering him.

"You okay?" I ask, looking up into his eyes.

"I'm better than okay, sweetheart."

I grin and decide not to press him further. We're out to have fun tonight, and we can talk about whatever's bothering him when we're alone.

When the song ends, we walk to the bar for another drink. Martini for me, more water for him. Out of the corner of my eye, I see someone stumble.

"Abby?" I frown as the nineteen-year-old just smiles over at me with glassy eyes. "Oh, Abs."

"Hey! Soph! I'm good."

"Good and wasted," Ike mutters as we approach her.

"Abby, you've been drinking."

"Psh." She waves me off but then giggles. "I only had a couple sips from drinks on the tables. It's only a little bit. Don't worry."

"You can't be drinking, Abby." I take her hand in mine so she doesn't rush away. "The club could get into a lot of trouble, and we won't even discuss how much shit you'll be in with your dad. You know, the *cop*."

"There's no need to tell my dad." She scowls now, and her face gets redder. "Don't be an asshole, Sophie. It's just a couple of sips."

"And that's not allowed, Abby. So yeah, that makes me an asshole." I flag Stella and Josie over as Abby actively tries to pull away from me. She succeeds and ends up flat on her ass.

"What's going on?" Stella asks and then tilts her head to the side. "Oh, someone's plowed."

"I am not," Abby says as she stands. "Sophie assaulted me."

I sputter and then laugh out loud.

"I'll call your dad," Josie says, taking her phone out of her bag, but Abby violently shakes her head and snatches Josie's phone out of her hand.

"No. Do *not* call him. I don't know why this is such a big deal. It was only a few sips."

"Enough to mess you up, and that's not cool. The underage crew knew the deal going into this," Stella says firmly. "We love being with you, but we don't supply you with alcohol. So yeah, we're calling your dad, and you can go home."

The music has stopped now, and the other cousins are circling around us.

"For fuck's sake, Abs." This comes from Finn, Abby's younger brother, and he looks damn pissed off. "Now you've screwed it up for the rest of us, and they won't invite us to the fun stuff anymore."

"Yeah, it's all about you," Abby spits at Finn. "God

forbid someone ruins anything for *you*."

"Okay, we're going to wait for Matt outside." I take Abby's hand again and lean in to whisper in her ear. "Do *not* say another word and ruin this for Olivia. Do you hear me? March your ass outside with me and get some fresh air."

She closes her mouth, and I guide her out the door. I can feel Ike behind us, and I appreciate him being there, having my back.

"I can't believe they called my dad."

Abby's wearing a simple, short dress, and she starts to shiver in the cool spring air.

Ike wraps his jacket around her.

"If you hadn't decided to drink when you absolutely know that's not cool, we wouldn't have. Besides, I can't believe you acted like a spoiled teenager and tried to ruin Olivia's night."

She's quiet for a minute, then shrugs a shoulder. "I just wanted to see what it was like."

"There's a time and place for everything, and this wasn't it. But part of being young is learning those things."

"My dad's gonna kill me."

"Maybe."

She looks at me with wide blue eyes, and her eyes fill with tears. "Will you talk to him?"

"Nope. Sorry, babe, you're gonna face the music on this one."

"Damn it." The tears are miraculously gone.

"You're a handful, aren't you?" Ike says with a laugh, speaking for the first time. "Don't let that get out of control and ruin a lot of things for you."

"You don't understand how much it sucks to be one of the youngest in this family. We're left out of everything; we don't get to have fun."

"Yeah, it's a tough life for you." I roll my eyes as Matt speeds up to the curb, and his brakes squeal as he stops.

When he gets out of the car and aims his intense, angry gaze at his daughter, even *I* feel nervous.

Not that he would ever hurt her. But yeah, there are going to be some consequences for this one.

"Get in the car."

"Daddy—"

"Not one word, Abigail. In the car."

She rolls her eyes and gets into the passenger seat, and Matt turns to me. "How bad?"

"Just bad enough to be a little too brave with her attitude and get a little sloppy."

"The attitude isn't new." He nods once, then narrows his eyes on Ike. "I don't know you."

"Ike." He offers his hand to shake. "Ike Harrison. Nice to meet you."

Matt's eyes move from Ike to me and then back to Ike. "Likewise. Is this a thing now?"

"Yeah," I reply with a sweet smile. "It's a thing. I love you. Don't kill her."

He gazes at Ike again, then leans in and kisses my cheek. "Love you back. See you later."

He gets back into his car and pulls away.

"Well, talk about family drama," I say brightly as I turn to Ike and lean into him. "Sorry about that. It's unusual for us."

"Are you kidding? I haven't been this entertained in ages."

I laugh, and we turn back to the club.

"What now?" he asks. "Do you want to keep dancing for a while?"

"Actually, I do. I want to dance, have one more drink, and enjoy some of the people I love the most in the world."

"Then that's what we'll do. Lead the way."

"How did we all end up on the floor?" I ask Stella, who's sitting next to me. We lost our shoes a long time ago. And now, there's a group of us girls on the floor, giggling like loons.

"Someone fell, someone else tried to help, and here we are," Stella says with a giggle. "It's really kind of comfy."

"We might get botulism," I reply. "Or mange. Or hepatitis."

"Which one?" Liv asks, staring at me through just one eye.

"Which one what?"

"Which hepatitis?"

I think about it for a minute and then shrug. "Does it matter?"

"Kinda." Liv closes both eyes. "I can't feel my lips. Does that mean I have mange? Oh my God, I'm getting married in a week! I can't have mange!"

"You don't have the mange, you have martiniitis." That's Maddie's voice. "I don't know if you can see it, but our guys are looking at us the way a tiger stares at a gazelle."

"What's a gazelle?" Josie wants to know.

"You know, those deer-like things. They're hungry. For *us*," Maddie replies.

"I'm gonna open my eye and see," Liv says. "Yep. They want us. You guys, Vaughn gives the *best* orgasms."

"Impossible," Stella says, waving her hand drunkenly. "Because Gray gives the best ones."

"But have you had one in an airplane bathroom?" Maddie asks with a giggle. "It's a whole new level of orgasm."

"Gray has a thing for elevators," Stella says with a smug smile. "And it doesn't suck, let me tell you."

"I used to have a stuffed animal," I begin, but Stella cuts me off with a snort.

"If you tell me that stuffy gave you good orgasms, you'll be excommunicated from this party."

"No. Ew. I named him 'Gasm because he had wild hair."

Everyone is quiet for a minute. "That's both cute and disturbing," Josie decides.

"I think they're coming," I alert the others.

"That's what *he* said," Liv replies and then snort laughs. "Get it?"

"I'm gonna need to have sex," I inform Ike as he approaches. He stops cold and looks surprised. "Like, right away."

"I mean, we're in public right now, sweetheart."

"When we're not in public."

"Same," Liv chimes in and reaches for Vaughn, who just lifts her right up off the floor. "All the sexy sex. Super sexy sex. SSS."

"Oh my God, we're wasted," Josie says and smiles goofily at her man, Brax. "Come on, let's do the SSS."

"Your wish is my command."

When we're up off the floor, and we've hugged and said goodbye to everyone, our guys pour us into waiting vehicles.

"We should go to my place," I inform Ike when he's at the wheel. "It's closer, and I need the SSS."

"I had no idea that alcohol made you this horny."

I grin over at him. "Well, duh. Don't you remember when I called you from the party, wanting it? But this time, I'm not too drunk. I'm just right. And I'm going to ride you like…I don't even know. But it's going to be a lot of fun."

"I can't wait."

He parks next to my car in the underground parking lot and helps me out of the truck so he can lead me to the elevator.

Once the doors are closed, I'm on him.

"I could just climb you like a goddamn tree." My hands are in his hair, and his are on my ass as I boost myself up to kiss him and rub myself all over him.

God, there are too many clothes involved.

The doors ding as they open on my floor, and he doesn't set me down. He just carries me right to my apartment.

He keys in the code to unlock the door and pushes inside.

"Couch," I say against his mouth.

"No." He carries me to the kitchen island and sets me on top. The stone countertop is cold on my ass, and he squats in front of me, parts my legs, tears my panties out of the way, and plants his mouth on me.

"Oh, shit." I lean back on my elbows, giving him better access. "Oh, hell yes. Have I mentioned how much I love your mouth?"

He moans against me, and the vibration is just amazing. It pushes me up the hill toward the promised land.

And then Ike yanks me off the counter, turns me around, and bends me over.

"Hard and fast," he pants against my ear. "Tell me if that's not what you want."

"I want it." I push my backside out more. "Hell yes, I want it."

I hear his zipper and the rustle of clothes, and then he's pushing into me, his hands firm on my hips as he pounds me hard, filling me so deliciously, I cry out his name.

My body is shivering in delight when he comes, and his groans make me shiver again.

Everything about this man is sexy as hell.

"Yeah, that's what I needed," I breathe against the counter. "I've needed it all day."

His hand glides from the back of my neck, down my spine, to my ass.

"You never have to ask me twice."

CHAPTER 12

IKE

"*W*hat's wrong?"

We've been lying in her bed for quite some time. I thought for sure she was asleep, after all the dancing, alcohol, and sex.

But it seems I was wrong.

I kiss her forehead softly. "Go to sleep."

"I can feel that something's off," she says and sits up, leans over, and flips on the bedside light. "Was my family too much for you tonight? I know they're a lot. Maybe we're not at the *meet the family* stage yet."

"Your cousins are great. I told you before, I'll gladly meet anyone you want me to. Hell, I already know your uncle pretty well." And it's the truth. Sure, I got the third degree a few times tonight from some of the cousins, but everyone was nice. "I was going to talk with you in the morning."

"I mean, if you're breaking up with me, which

sounds super dramatic because it's not even like we've established that we're in a committed relationship or anything, I guess it's good that we had some great sex tonight."

I move swiftly and pin her beneath me on the bed, kissing the hell out of her.

And when I come up for air, I can see the confusion and hurt swimming in those gorgeous blue eyes.

"Let's get something straight. We're in a committed relationship. I'm absolutely *not* breaking up with you. For fuck's sake, Soph, I'm completely addicted to you."

The hurt leaves, and it's replaced with a happy smile.

"Oh, good. Same goes. So, tell me what's wrong. I've sensed it all night."

Is it nuts that we've only known each other for such a short time, and yet she can already read me so well?

Maybe.

I sit up and push my hands through my hair, blow out a breath, and gather my thoughts.

"I have to go to Oklahoma tomorrow."

"*Tomorrow?*"

"Yeah." I nod my head and look over at her. She doesn't look mad or frustrated. She just looks *concerned.* "Family stuff. I told you my dad would cause a fuss when he found out about the new contract."

"And he's causing a fuss."

"Yeah. He is. He's not a good person, Sophie. And he

thinks I owe him everything. That I should keep just enough to scrape by and give him the rest."

"Absofuckinglutely *not*."

Her face is mutinous, and I lean over to kiss her nose. "Agreed. I did that for a while because I thought that was normal. But, after talking with the other guys, Will, and the financial planners, I've learned otherwise. So, I get to go have a really uncomfortable conversation with my old man."

"I'm coming with you."

"No." I immediately shake my head and reach for her hand, link our fingers, and kiss her knuckles. "Thank you for wanting to. But no. It's not going to be a pretty scene, and I won't have my dad say shit about you, to your face or behind your back. Because he's gonna be damn pissed, and he'll lash out at you. He will *not* have that satisfaction."

She sighs but doesn't argue. "I seriously hate this for you."

"I should have stood up to him a long time ago."

"What about your mom?"

"She's why I never stood my ground, to be honest. She's so bullied and broken down, and she's the one who has to face his wrath whenever something doesn't go his way. So, yeah, I put up with a lot from him and gave him way more money than I should have, for her. But not anymore. I'm going to offer to take her out of there. And I need you to know that if she wants to come back to Washington with me, I'll bring her."

"Of course, you will. Do you think that would be a bad thing for me, knowing how family oriented I am?"

"No, but I'm not going to assume anything at all. She's my mom. And I can't leave her there with him unless she insists on staying."

"Which she might do," Sophie says softly. "She might not think she's strong enough to leave."

"I'm hoping that's not the case."

"When do you fly out?"

"The plane leaves at nine. I'll just leave my truck at the airport while I'm gone."

"Bullshit." She stares at me like I've just told her I'm going to drive it off of a cliff. "I'll take you to the airport. And I'll pick you up. Anything you need."

I pull her against me, and we lie back down, snuggled together. "Thank you. Honestly, thanks a lot."

"It's nothing."

But she's wrong. It's everything. I don't know that anyone has ever been this quick to jump in and help, to be so understanding.

Not only is Sophie gorgeous and smart, but she's special, as well, and I'll do everything I can to keep her in my life.

Would I like to have her come to Oklahoma with me? Sure. I'd love for my mom to meet her. I think they'd get along great.

But my dad will not have the opportunity to swipe at her. I'll protect her from that at all costs.

"It's all going to work out," she says, her voice sleepy

now, and she cuddles up closer, kissing my chest. "Don't worry."

But I lie here in the dark and listen to her breathe. Yeah, I'm worried.

But it needs to be done.

"Hey, Mom."

Her arms are open wide as she hurries to me and hugs me close.

"Welcome home, baby."

I texted her this morning to tell her that I was flying in, and she insisted on picking me up. I'm glad because I want to give her a heads-up before I talk to Dad.

"You didn't tell Dad?" I ask when we've put my bag in the back of her car, and she's driving toward the house I bought my parents just outside of Oklahoma City. Dad sold the farm, said he didn't want that life anymore, and he and Mom now live in the suburbs.

"No, but I'm not sure why your being here is a secret." She glances at me with concerned eyes. "Did you lose the contract?"

"No." I shake my head and feel my stomach tighten when her shoulders visibly sag in relief. "Why?"

"I just thought maybe you wanted to deliver some bad news in person, that's all."

"I do, but it's not because I lost my contract. Mom, things are about to change, big time. And I don't want you to be blindsided because I know that you're always the one that he takes everything out on."

"You know that Clark is an emotional man—"

"No, Mom. He's an asshole."

"Isaiah Harrison, I will not have you speaking about your father like that."

"I'm an adult, and I'm just speaking the truth. You know it, too. You *know*, Mom."

She tightens her lips together but doesn't respond for a long time.

"I'm done giving him money," I say softly.

"What?" Now her eyes are full of fear. "You're cutting us off?"

"Not you," I reply and reach over to touch her shoulder. "Never you. But him? Yeah. It's not right that he bleeds me dry, Mom. Most of what he does isn't right. You didn't want to move off the farm. You didn't want that huge house in the suburbs that you have to take care of."

"It's a beautiful house." Her voice is a little softer, a little more unsure. "I don't have anything to complain about, and you know it."

"I know that Clark Harrison is a bully and that he's mean to you more than he's kind. He's been taking me for granted, wasting a shit ton of money, and it's over. He's done. He's young and able-bodied. If he's gotten himself into trouble financially, he'll have to figure out how to dig himself out of it."

Mom just nods and then takes a long, deep breath.

"I've been thinking the same for a long time, Ike. You're right. What he's done is a shame, and he has acted like he's the one who's worked so hard for all that money. He's a selfish man."

"I need you to know that I'm not leaving you here with him, Mom."

Now she laughs. "And just where will I go?"

"Wherever you want." I shrug and watch as she takes the exit toward their house. "I know that Aunt Suzie's in that retirement community in Florida. You always said that someday you two would be old ladies together."

"Who are you calling an old lady, young man?"

I grin at her now. "You know what I mean. Or, you're more than welcome at my place in Washington. I'm sure Nellie would love to have you with her, as well. You have so many people who want you, Mom."

She nibbles her lip, clearly thinking it over.

"Give me a day or so to think it over," she finally says and then swallows hard. "You'll help me? You won't make me do it alone if I decide to go?"

"Mom, I will be here as long as you need me."

She nods as she pulls into the driveway, and a new wave of rage rolls through me.

"He still bought the truck?"

There's a brand-new Chevy sitting in the driveway with temporary tags on it.

"He always finds a way," she says, but there's no pride or joy in her voice. "Yeah, he talked the dealer

179

into letting him leave with it, and they'll figure out the payment in a few days, *once he talks some sense into you*, he says."

"He's about to be sorely disappointed."

We start toward the house, but Mom stops with a frown. "Aren't you bringing your bag inside?"

"No, ma'am. I'm not staying here."

She pauses, then nods, and I follow her up to the front door and inside the house. I can hear Dad in the kitchen, but he hasn't seen us yet.

"Where the fuck did you go?" he demands, instantly putting my back up. "I didn't say you could go shopping or anything and spend my fucking money. I had to make my own goddamn sandwich. What good are you if you're never here to take care of me? It's always the same old shit with you."

God, I hate him.

"I didn't go shopping," Mom says as we round the corner to the kitchen.

Dad stops short, having just finished licking the mustard off a butter knife, and his scowl turns into a smile when he sees me.

"Well, I'll be damned. Welcome home, son! Did you come home to celebrate our new contract? Hell of a thing, isn't it?"

He sets the knife aside and rounds the island to me, pulling me in for a manly, shoulder-slapping hug.

His body has gotten softer since I last saw him. The beer belly has grown, and his muscles have atrophied. He's in his late-fifties and living a life of leisure.

"Damn, it's good to see you. Melanie, make us something to eat, why don'tcha?"

"No, it's okay, Mom. I need to talk to you, Dad."

His eyes narrow on me, and the first film of ice forms over his face.

"All right. Let's go into the living room and talk. Come on, Mel."

"Just you and me," I reply and look back to wink at my mom.

She already has her phone in hand. I hope she's about to call her sister while I take care of this with Dad because, after that little display, there's no way in hell that I'm leaving her here. No way.

"Okay." He leads me into the living room with big leather recliners and a ridiculously huge TV hanging on one wall. "What do you think of that? I needed something bigger to watch your games on."

"You'll be able to see my nose hair on that thing."

Dad laughs and nods, then sits in his recliner like a king on his throne.

"What's on your mind, son?"

"I want to start this by saying that I hope you can return that fancy new truck in the driveway."

His face turns red, but he doesn't speak. Not yet.

"You don't have the money for it."

"I'm about to have *millions*."

"From where?"

He sputters and leans forward. "Don't tell me you fucked up and got fired without pay."

"*I'm* not the one who has fucked up," I reply evenly. "Yes, I'm earning a very good paycheck. *I* am, Dad. Not you."

"Why, you ungrateful little fuck."

"No, you don't get to do that to me anymore. I'm not ungrateful, and we both know it. I've handed over *millions* to you. Not to mention, you made a hell of a bunch of money off the sale of the farm but didn't bother to put it towards this house."

"That's *my* money."

"Right. Well, here's some truth for you, Dad. This house? It's in *my* name. I'm going to sign it over to you, and it's the last thing I'm going to give you."

"I can't afford the taxes on this dump!"

I simply stare at him for a long minute, and then I laugh my ass off. "Well, then I guess you can sell it and buy something else that you can afford. I bailed you out of a lot of shit, Dad. I had you debt free, with a beautiful home and truck, and pretty much whatever you needed, but that wasn't enough. You've managed to siphon off every single dime of that first contract."

"I'm *entitled.*"

"No, you're not. You're just not."

"So, you're just going to keep four hundred million dollars to yourself and let your mother and me starve?"

"No. Not at all. Mom won't want for anything. And

let's be honest, you're not exactly starving here. You'll figure it out."

"I can't believe I raised you to be a selfish son of a bitch."

"Why not? I learned it from you."

He couldn't look more surprised if I punched him in the face. "You little bastard."

"Enough."

This comes from Mom in the doorway. We both look her way, and I'm pleased to see her hands on her hips and her face set firmly.

"You won't speak to my son that way. He's spoken his mind, and he has a right to feel the way he does. Maybe if you hadn't been so greedy, it wouldn't be this way, Clark."

"This is none of your business, you ugly bitch."

"And, we're done." I narrow my eyes at him before I walk to Mom and drape my arm over her shoulders, but she just pats my hand and steps forward.

Dad's panting and has wild eyes.

"If you take a swing at her, it'll be the last thing you ever do."

"Did you tattle?" he demands of my mom. "Did you go crying to Ike and tattle about all the little things I've done like I'm in *trouble*? Jesus, Mel, I only hit you once, and you deserved it!"

I want to kill him. I want to rip out his throat and watch him gasp for air until he dies.

But Mom just calmly shakes her head no.

"I didn't say a word about all the times you've *spanked* me, as you put it, or called me filthy names. Given me the silent treatment. But I'm telling you right now, I'm done. I'm leaving."

Now he laughs. "Oh, yeah? Where the fuck are you going to go?"

"It doesn't matter. I won't be here. I won't be your outlet for anger anymore."

"Now, honey, I think you need to calm down. Don't worry about Ike not giving us money anymore. I'll figure it out. You don't have to go; you know I'll always take care of you."

I snort, Mom sighs, and Dad stares at me with feral eyes.

"You talked her into this."

"He reminded me that I have options, and staying here isn't the only one I have. We've been married for thirty-five years, Clark. And for more than thirty of them, you've treated me like a slave, like a whore, and a punching bag. And I have way more worth than that."

"Fine." Dad stomps away. "Go. Get the fuck out. But I'm telling you right now, you won't get a dime out of me. You won't get half of this house when I sell it off."

"I don't need or want it," she says. "I have my own money."

Dad's eyes go to steel.

"That's right. I have my *own* money that you can't touch either. And I'll be just fine. I'm leaving today."

Wow, once she made up her mind, she didn't dilly-dally. I've never been more proud of someone than I am of my mom right now.

It just shows me that things have been far worse than I ever knew, and I wish I'd been man enough to do something about it sooner.

"Good. I don't want to look at either of you."

When we turn to go, I see that Mom already has three big suitcases and two small bags sitting by the door.

When I look at her in surprise, she simply shrugs. "I've been prepared for a long time."

"Mom, you have so much here in this house. You can't just leave with these suitcases."

"He sold all of my parents' antiques," she says softly. "I had all the family photos converted to digital. I have a few of your and Nellie's baby things, my clothes, and my mother's recipe book. Everything that's dear to me is here."

"Are you sure? I have no problem gathering your stuff and shipping it."

She nods. "I just want to *go.*"

I load up her things into her car and pull away.

"Where are we going?" I ask her.

"Florida," she replies happily. "I know it's a spontaneous road trip, but while you were talking to your dad, I called Aunt Suzie, and she told me that if I didn't take you up on your offer of help and get my little ass to her house *right now*, she would come pick me up herself."

The lead that's been sitting in my stomach all day loosens.

"I just have to swing by the bank," I tell her. "Tie a few loose ends. Then, we're Florida-bound."

"How exciting." She settles down in her seat, but I see that her hands are shaking.

"Mom, are you okay?"

When she looks my way again, her eyes are full of tears. "I'm going to be just fine, honey. I think I'm relieved more than anything."

"If I'd known that it was that bad with him all these years, I would have done something sooner."

"Now, don't you go blaming yourself, my sweet boy. Sometimes, life is just hard. It wasn't a horrible life with him, you know. Yes, there were awful moments, but for the most part, I just did my own thing. Especially these last few years. The past couple of weeks weren't fun because he was frustrated that you wouldn't just dump a pile of money in his account."

"And he takes his frustrations out on you."

"Always. But not anymore. I don't know the first thing about filing for divorce, but I'll figure it out."

"*We* will," I reply. "I'll hire you an amazing lawyer. I'll pay for your apartment at Aunt Suzie's place and set you up with an account."

"That's really not necessary, although I do appreciate the offer. I've managed to save more than six figures over the years, just waiting for the moment to leave him."

I stare over at her. "That's a lot of money, Mom."

"I know."

"But it won't last forever. I bet that apartment isn't cheap."

"Well, if I need help, I'll let you know. Maybe I'll let you buy me a new couch."

"And a bed?"

"No. I'm going to buy that for myself. I think a woman needs to do that."

"Okay. I'm so proud of you, Mom."

She smiles. "I'm proud of the both of us, baby."

CHAPTER 13

SOPHIE

*H*e's been gone a week, but it feels like *years.*

I've been good about not texting him too much or acting like I can't live without him. Because I *can* live without him.

I just don't want to.

I know he's dealing with a lot of stuff with his family. He's been moving his mom into a new apartment in Florida so she can be close to her sister.

I mean, he's helping his *mom* get out of an abusive situation, for the love of Moses, so it's not like I can really complain. I don't *want* to complain.

But I'd just gotten used to having him around, to being with him so much, and then he left on this trip.

And I miss him.

"Earth to Sophie."

I turn to Becs and raise an eyebrow. "Yeah?"

"For God's sake, when does the sexy quarterback come back?"

"I don't know. I haven't heard from him in a few days." I shrug a shoulder, trying to act nonchalant. "He'll be home when he's finished with everything that needs him there."

She nods. "Well, I hope it's soon because you've been *moody as fuck* since he left."

"I have not."

"Right. Snapping at me because I didn't wash the grapes this morning *isn't* moody."

"Okay, that was a bad moment. I'm sorry for that."

"You *never* snap, so I know you're missing him. It's okay. If I was doing the bump and grind with the delicious Ike, I'd be missing him, too. I bet he has an excellent penis."

"You're so classy." But she made me laugh, and I didn't realize how badly I needed that. "And maybe a little perverted."

"Oh, honey, you haven't seen anything." Becs laughs as she wipes down my countertop. "Seriously, though, you've seemed sad. Don't worry, no one would notice, especially not in your videos, but I *know* you, and I can see it."

"I'm not *sad*," I reply thoughtfully and tap my lips as I think about it. "I'm really proud of him for taking care of his mom and for standing up to his deadbeat dad. I think, more than anything, I'm lonely for him. Which is so silly because I've only known him for a few weeks, but we'd already started to meld into each other's lives, and I got used to it, you know?"

"Yeah, you're a routine girl, for sure. Sometimes, I wonder if you're seventy."

"I'm not sure how to respond to that."

"Hey, I love you, even if you act like an old lady sometimes. Doesn't bother me at all. You miss him. Nothing wrong with that."

Now I'll be thinking about the fact that Becs thinks I act like a senior citizen all day. I won't have time to worry about when Ike's coming home.

"Okay, friend, I have to go. I have about twelve hours of film to cut down to three-minute vids, a plethora of photos to edit, and you have a bunch of emails, too."

"I know. I'm planning to make myself some tea and sit down with the laptop this afternoon. I can't wait to see what you do with that footage. You should do a bloopers reel. The viewers love that."

"We haven't done that in a while. You got it. Do you need anything else? I'm going to be out of town next week."

"I haven't forgotten," I reply with a wink. "Go. Enjoy your Hawaiian vacation. You totally deserve it."

She does a little happy dance, and then she's off. We've worked double the hours this week so that I have plenty of content next week while Becs is gone. The viewers won't be any the wiser.

I've just set the water on the stove to boil when my phone rings.

My heart leaps when I see Ike's name.

"Hey," I say into the phone. "How's it going?"

"God, it's good to hear your voice." He sounds tired. "I'm good. Really good, actually. It's been a crazy week, but Mom's all settled in her new place, with new furniture and everything."

"That was fast."

"I might have bribed the owner of the store with a signed jersey if he would put a rush on delivery."

"Nice flex." I grin and pour the hot water over my tea bag. "Is her new place cute?"

"Yeah, it is, actually. Not huge, but she has two bedrooms and two bathrooms, and she's just down the hall from her sister. They're excited to be together."

"I'm surprised you were able to find her a place so fast, in exactly the building she wanted."

"Me, too. It had just opened up, and I snagged it. I'm telling you, it all came together perfectly, as if it were just meant to be."

"Because it was. Any word from your dad?"

He sighs, and I wish I could reach out and hug him.

"I haven't heard from him, but Mom has. He calls or texts her incessantly. He doesn't know how to do anything, Soph. Laundry, dishes, even the fucking lawn. None of it. She has been his slave. The last time he called, she suggested he hire a housekeeper and hung up on him."

"Good for her. Ike, I really hope he doesn't cause problems for her, like trying to track her down and hurt her."

"He won't," he says, and I can hear the conviction in his voice. "He's tried to coerce her into coming home, but he's just bruised more than anything. His pride is hurt. He doesn't love my mom. He doesn't give a shit if he's married to her. What he cares about most is the money. As fucked-up as it sounds, I honestly think he's more heartbroken over me cutting him off than he is about losing his wife."

"That's just...sad," I decide with a frown.

"It's pathetic. But I have good news."

"What's that?"

"I'm on my way home."

I stop stirring my tea and feel my heart climb into my throat. "Really? Right now?"

"Yep. I'm about to board the flight to Seattle."

"When do you land? I'll pick you up!"

"Actually, I have a ride, but I was kind of hoping you might want to meet me at my place. I've missed you, sweetheart."

I sigh happily. "I'll be there. I've missed you, too. What do you need? Should I cook? Do you need me to clean up anything?"

"Pam's there today, so it'll be clean, but thanks for offering. I just need you, baby."

"You've got me. Shoot me your flight number so I can stalk the plane. I'm excited to see you."

"I like the sound of that. Okay. I better go. They're calling my group now."

"Have a safe flight, and I'll see you soon."

"Bye, beautiful."

"Bye." I hang up and jump up and down excitedly. "Oh my God, he's coming home! Okay, I'm gonna pour this in a to-go mug and go over to his place. I can take my laptop. I'll make him dinner."

With that decided, I gather my things and load it all up in my backpack, grab the insulated cup full of tea, and set off.

I get to see my man in just a few hours.

THE GROCERY STORE was surprisingly empty today, and I was able to take my time gathering everything I need. I could have gone the fancy route, but Ike's going to be exhausted. A day of traveling is tiring enough, but add in the emotional family stuff, and it's just a *lot.*

So, I went with comfort food. I'm going to make a healthy and delicious lasagna with bread, and I decided to throw caution to the wind and make him some carrot cake for dessert.

Carrots are vegetables, so that's healthy, too.

I key in the code on the pad to drive through his gate, and when I pull up to the house, I see a car that must be his housekeeper, Pam's.

I don't want to be in her way, but I'm just so excited

to be here, so I grab some bags of groceries and walk through the front door.

"Hello?"

I can hear a vacuum running upstairs, which means she can't hear me.

"Good, I'm not in her way." I cross to the kitchen, pleased to see that she's already finished up in here, and get to work putting away groceries, then walk out to my car for the last few bags.

When I'm on my way back in, Pam's just coming down the stairs and screams when she sees me.

"Oh my God!" She almost slips but grabs on to the railing.

"Oh, shit! I'm so sorry! I'm Sophie."

"Scared me," she says and pats her chest. "I thought I heard someone, but I wasn't expecting...anyway. Hello there. Is Ike home?"

"No, he's on a plane here now. I thought I'd come over and cook him dinner. He's expecting me."

Pam smiles and walks down the rest of the stairs. "He told me that he'd been dating someone. You're quite beautiful."

I blink at her and then feel my cheeks flush. "Thank you. Will I be in your way if I putter around in the kitchen?"

"Not at all. I'm just finishing up. I was going to put something in the oven for him, but it looks like you'll be saving me that step. The boy needs to eat more home-cooked meals."

"I've been doing some of that for him since we've been dating. I'm a nutritionist."

"Well, hallelujah. You go ahead and putter around, dear. Just call me if you need me."

"Same goes, thanks."

Pam goes back to work, and I get settled in the kitchen. First, I open my laptop at the round kitchen table in the nook and key in his flight information so I can see how long he has before he lands.

We're *really* far from Florida. It's at least a five-hour flight, maybe longer, so I have plenty of time before I have to get the lasagna in the oven. Sure enough, he lands in three hours.

Then there's another hour from the airport to his place, with traffic.

So, rather than get started cooking, I decide to get some work done first. If I can crack down and focus for a little while, I'll be able to shift that focus to Ike for the rest of the night.

And he's all I want to think about once he's home.

"Lasagna, check. Bread, check. Salad and cake, check."

I've managed to get all my work done, get food ready, and get the cake baked and frosted, all before Ike gets home.

It's good that I had so much to do because I've been a ball of nerves. Excited nerves, but still.

Now, he just needs to *get here.*

For the sixtieth time, I walk to the front door and stare out the window, and finally, headlights beam up the driveway.

"Yay!" I fling the door open and do a little cha-cha on the threshold. Ike steps out of the passenger side, and I see one of his teammates in the driver's seat. They say something to each other, exchange a fist bump, and then Ike takes his bag out of the back seat and turns to walk toward me.

I don't wait for him. I just run down the steps and leap into his arms.

I hear the *thud* of his bag hitting the pavement and the car leaving down the driveway, but all I can feel is *Ike.*

"I'm *so* glad to see you," I say into his neck as I cling to him.

"This is the best homecoming I've ever had." I can hear the smile in his voice, and I lean back so I can see him. "Hey, sweetheart."

"Hey. I'm glad you're home."

"I figured." He kisses me now, long and slow. "You're a sight for sore eyes."

"Come on. Let's get you inside and settled." I reach for his bag, but he shoos me out of the way and takes it himself. "You didn't take much for being away a week."

"I had to do laundry twice," he says with a laugh. "I definitely should have planned better. Something smells *really* good in here."

"Lasagna's in the oven, ready whenever you are. I even baked a cake. I had some nervous energy to get rid of while I waited for you."

"I'm starving," he says. He hasn't stopped touching me, and it's like a balm to my soul. "But will it keep long enough for a shower?"

"Sure. Go ahead, and I'll set the temp on low."

He sets off upstairs, and I hurry to the kitchen to make sure that everything will keep for another thirty minutes or so, and then I race after him.

If he thinks he gets to take a shower alone, he's got another thing coming.

The water's already running in the bathroom. His bag is open on the bed, and when I walk into the bathroom, Ike's just putting away his toothbrush.

"I always feel gross after riding on an airplane," he says and then turns to me. I thought we might have playful sex in the water, but I know now that's not what he needs.

So, I walk behind him and kiss his shoulder before nudging his shirt up and over his head, then tossing it in the nearby hamper.

There won't be any clothes-tearing, desperate, hurried sex this time.

No, I'm going to take care of him. I'm going to *love* him.

With my eyes on his in the mirror, I kiss all over his bare shoulder and reach around to unzip his jeans. He helps me get the denim over his hips and down his legs, and as steam begins to fill the room, he turns to me and frames my face in his hands.

"I missed you so fucking much."

I smile up at him and run my hands up and down his sides, enjoying the way his smooth skin and sculpted muscles feel against my skin. "Same. But I'm glad you took the trip."

"Me, too. I'm glad it's over. Now I'm here, and I just want to lose myself in you tonight, Soph."

"Yeah, that's the plan."

He kisses me, long and slow, making my toes curl. And when he gently removes my sweater and my leggings, leading me into the shower with him, I don't object in the least.

We take our time soaping each other up, as if we're rediscovering each other's bodies all over again.

But I haven't forgotten his. I remember exactly how he looks, how he feels, and how he reacts when I touch him.

I kneel before him and watch the water sluice over his perfect body, leaving rivers down his skin.

His cock hardens in front of my eyes, and I can't resist cupping him in my hands, feeling him.

First, I take my time washing him. I love the way he slips and slides through my hands with the soap, and when I've rinsed his skin clean, I lean in and taste him.

He smells of his soap, but his essence is still there, and it turns me on in ways I've never felt before.

"Fucking hell," he groans and leans in to brace his

hands on the tile wall. That only makes me feel bolder, *sexier*, and I lick and suck, pull and entice until he suddenly swears again and pulls me to my feet.

"You undo me." His lips are on my neck as he reaches down, palms my ass, and lifts me against the wall. We seem to really love shower sex because we end up here often.

And I'm not complaining.

But I feel the shift this time. When he fills me, he pauses and stares into my eyes. God, I want to tell him that I love him so damn bad.

But is it too soon? Is it totally stupid to say it for the first time when we're having sex?

I don't know.

Instead, I cup his face in my hands and rub my nose over his before kissing him sweetly, and he starts to move. Long, easy strokes that feel like he's massaging every inch of me. I can't help but clench around him, making us both moan.

"Can't get enough of you," he says softly. "It's never enough."

"I'm right here." He begins to move faster, finally chasing after that glorious orgasm, and I move my hips with him. Until, finally, we're both coming apart together. "Looks like I have to wash you off again."

"Hell no," he says with a laugh. "We'll never make it out of here, and I'm starving."

"Let's go eat, then, and I'll fill you in on my week."

"Deal."

Ike dries us both off, something he seems to enjoy and I will never say no to, and then we dress in fresh clothes before we head down to the kitchen.

"Did you make *carrot* cake?" he asks.

"Yes, and the icing too, all from scratch. It's my grandma's recipe."

"I'm warning you," he says as he sniffs the cake. "This is my favorite, and I might only save you one tiny piece."

I laugh and swat his ass with my dish towel. "I'll fight you for it. It's my favorite, too."

"You'll probably win," he says with a wink. "You're pretty badass."

"I totally am." I pull the lasagna and bread out of the oven, and Ike pulls down plates for us. "But no need to fight. There's plenty here."

"Let's go eat in the living room by the fireplace," he suggests. "It's cozy in there."

"Let's do it," I agree, and we carry our plates and glasses of wine into the living room. Ike flips on the gas fireplace, and we sit on the floor with our plates in our laps and dig in.

"So damn good," he mumbles around his food. "Holy shit, you can cook."

"It's my job." I shrug and eat my own food. "I want to show people that you don't have to eat stuff that's tasteless or just plain gross in order to eat well. Sure, there's cheese in this, but there are also a ton of veggies and protein. And I made the bread from scratch with gluten-free flour."

"This is gluten-free?" he asks. "No way. It doesn't taste like cardboard."

"Exactly."

"You're a fucking genius." He takes another bite. "Okay, tell me everything that I missed this week."

CHAPTER 14

IKE

"*Y*ou have a really great backyard," Sophie says the next morning. We decided to have coffee on the back porch, with views of the water and my yard.

"We sound like adults," I reply and sip from my mug. She's sitting in her own chair, but her legs are propped up on my thighs, and I'm rubbing the arch of one of her feet.

"I hate to break it to you, but we *are* adults, Isaiah."

"Wow, you broke out the full name. Does that mean I'm in trouble?"

"No, it means you're a grown-up." She smirks and then looks out over my estate once again. "I like it out here. You have a big, fenced grassy area, and that fire pit is killer. Have you ever used it?"

"No."

She goggles at me, and I shrug. "I keep meaning to,

but I just haven't had the occasion. I'm not really one to sit by the fire by myself."

"Well, if you don't hate the idea, I'd like to invite some of the cousins over and have a barbecue out here, enjoy that fire pit. Maybe play some cornhole. Although, they get pretty competitive."

"I can handle that. I'm competitive for a living, sweetheart."

"I know." She grins and leans her head back on the chair. "You need a dog in this backyard."

"Can't happen."

"Why not?"

"I'm gone way too much. I don't want to have to put them at a boarding kennel all the damn time. It's just not fair."

"But you *want* a dog."

I shrug a shoulder and reach for my fork to take a bite of the leftover carrot cake.

Breakfast of champions.

"Who doesn't want a dog? Hell, I'd have four dogs and as many cats as my house can hold if I could."

"Okay, now that might be a bit much."

I laugh and offer her a bite of the carrot cake, which she happily takes. "Don't tell me you're not an animal person."

"Oh, I definitely am. I would love a dog, but the condo isn't great for that. I *could* do it, but I'm like you in that I want to bring an animal to the best possible scenario. But, I don't plan to be in the condo forever. Just for now."

"Where do you plan to go?"

I want to tell her to just go ahead and move her shit into my place right now.

But I don't.

"I don't know. Someday, in the not-so-distant future, I'd love to have a house. I'd like to have my own vegetable and herb garden. Do you think I act like an old lady?"

I blink at the quick switch in conversation. "No, I was just kidding. We *should* be adults."

"No, like, do you think I always act like I'm in my seventies?"

"Trust me, babe, a seventy-year-old woman can't do what you did in bed this morning."

But she doesn't smile. She looks worried.

"I'm being serious," she says.

"So am I. Where is this coming from?"

"Yesterday, before you got home, Becs said that I have routines and stuff like a senior citizen, and I'm not even thirty yet."

"Wait. How old *are* you?"

She narrows her eyes at me. "I'm only twenty-eight."

"Uh-oh."

"What?"

"You're older than me."

"Not by much. Wait, how old are *you*?"

"You never googled me? I'm offended."

She rolls her eyes and just stares at me, waiting.

"I'm a quarter of a century."

"You're *twenty-five*? Jesus, I'm robbing the cradle, Ike."

I laugh and pull her foot back into my lap when she pulled away. "I'm not a kid. What's three stupid years?"

"I mean, it's a *lot.*"

I'm quiet for a moment as we both stare out at the water, watching the fog roll over the shoreline.

"They're paying a twenty-five-year-old guy close to half a *billion* dollars," I say softly. "Not all at once, but still."

"They wouldn't pay you that if you weren't worth it," she reminds me and leans over to take my hand. "Obviously, you make that and more back for the team. You undervalue how popular you are, Ike. And the fact that you're humble is something that I really love about you, but you have to know your worth. If they're willing to pay that, it means that, when it comes to ticket sales, jersey and other merchandise sales, etcetera, you make them more than that."

I swallow hard and look over at her. God, she's fucking gorgeous, sitting out here on my porch with me. I've never thought about sitting out here before, but here we are, at eight in the morning, soaking up the fresh air.

"It's staggering," I admit. "And mind-blowing."

"I know I said it before, but I'm going to say it again.

I'm really, *really* proud of you. I love that you don't feel entitled, that you're modest about your popularity and that you're just a nice guy."

"I'm not nice," I say, thinking about one of our earlier conversations, and grin. "Do you need me to remind you just how *not* nice I can be?"

She laughs now and pulls away to sit back in her chair. "You reminded me just fine this morning. So, what's on tap for you today?"

"I'm headed to the training facility to work out with some of the guys and catch up on anything that I missed while I was gone. Then, I volunteer at the shelter."

She frowns at me, and I realize that I haven't told her about this yet.

"What shelter?"

"Every week, I spend a few hours at one of the animal shelters to help out."

Sophie's quiet for a second, and then she clears her throat. "Okay, let me get this straight. You help your mom, you're ridiculously hot, but you don't act like a jerk about it, *and* you help take care of animals in the little spare time you have."

"So, you think I'm hot?"

She stands now and just climbs right into my lap, wraps her arms around my neck, and hugs me tightly.

"If I'd known I would get a hug out of it, I would have told you about the shelter sooner."

"Ike, I'm going to say something to you that I've

wanted to say for a little while, but I thought it might be too soon."

I nudge her back so I can see her face and cup her cheek in my hand, rubbing my thumb over the apple of her cheek.

"What is it?"

"I'm sure that I'm falling in love with you. I've been all up in my feelings about it, but I'm not really one to keep my mouth shut about these things."

"Thank God I'm not the only one feeling it."

"You do?" Those baby blues widen as if she's surprised, and I can't resist kissing her lightly. "Oh, yeah. I've never met anyone like you, Soph. You've overcome so much, you're an amazing business owner, and you're absolutely gorgeous. I love every thought in your head and every curve of your spectacular body."

"A lot of people would say that I shouldn't be your type. Physically, that is."

"Who are these *people*?" I ask, totally annoyed. "They're not in our bed. They're not in our relationship. Who gives one wild fuck what they think?"

"Not you, apparently."

"No, not me. And I already took care of the one person who had an issue, so it doesn't matter."

Her face stills, and I know without a doubt that I just fucked up.

"What? Who had a problem with us?"

"It doesn't matter, Soph."

"I want to know. No one in my family has said anything, and trust me, they would."

"No, not your family." I blow out a breath and twist a strand of her soft, dark hair around my finger. "Florence threw a little fit about it."

"Florence, your *boss*?"

"Yeah. She tried to have it written into my contract that I couldn't date you."

Now her mouth drops open, and she sputters. "W-what?"

"I told her I would never sign that. We were prepared to turn down the contract and go to another city."

"Wait." She scoots out of my lap and paces the porch. "Your boss hates our family enough to have it written into your contract that you're forbidden to date me."

"Which I *didn't* sign."

"This is such bullshit. We didn't do anything to her! It's exactly the opposite."

"Yeah, about that... I'm dying to know. What did she do?"

Sophie spins and gazes at me with hot eyes. "She fucked over Stella, big time. Florence hired her to redecorate her house here. Stella did everything that Florence said she wanted, and then when it was reveal day, Florence tore it apart *on camera*. Humiliated Stella live on social media, refused to pay for it, and got her fired."

"Damn," I mutter, shaking my head.

"Stella ended up suing, and won. She was reimbursed for the money she invested in the rehab, which was well over a quarter of a million dollars. And her former employer had to pay her restitution for wrongful termination. All of that was finally settled shortly after the first of the year."

"I'm glad that Stella won. She should. Florence is such a bitch, and we all hate that she owns the team. But, she does. There's nothing I can do about that. However, I made it clear that if she wants me to stay, there would be no clause mentioning your family. After a short game of chicken, she folded and took it out."

"Jesus, Ike, I'm *so sorry.*"

"Why?" I stand and cross to her now. "Why would you be sorry? It wasn't your fault at all."

"It's absolutely ridiculous that she would use *me* as leverage in your contract." She doesn't fight me when I tug her into my arms and hug her close, rocking her back and forth. "After everything Will has done for that team, she would turn around and do something like *this?*"

"Hey, it's under control now."

"I wish you'd told me when it happened."

She scowls up at me. "We were new, and Florence only found out that we were dating because someone took a picture of us at the market that day. It was our *second* date, Soph. Florence threw her fit, and I stood my ground with her. It seems I'm all about that this month."

She finally gives me a small smile. "Yeah, you are. What other cities were you looking into?"

"San Francisco and Denver were at the top of the list. Short flights to get here to you, to be honest. But my agent would say it's because they had the best deals on the table."

She kisses my chin. "Thank you for protecting us."

"I may be younger, but I'm not a kid, and I'm not stupid, Soph. I know a good thing when it takes me out in the park. I'm not letting you go for anyone. Not even for half a billion dollars."

"I think *I* would dump me for that much money."

"Not a chance." I kiss the top of her head and breathe her in. "Do you have to work today?"

"Just a little. Not too much. Why?"

"Can I talk you into going to the animal shelter with me? I promise not to make you clean up any poop. I'll do that."

"I'd love to. But I'm warning you, I'll want to bring them all home."

"It's a weekly problem for me."

"Hey there," Rhonda says with a bright smile as I walk into the shelter with Sophie in tow. "You brought a friend."

"I did. Rhonda, this is my girlfriend, Sophie."

"Holy shit," is all Rhonda says when she gets a good look at my girl. "Holy freaking shit."

"Hi," Sophie says with a wave.

"I *know* you," Rhonda says, then shakes her head. "Not in person, but I follow you on social media. My God, you helped me out of a really bad time in my life, and you didn't even know it. I was just getting out of a bad marriage. I felt fat and ugly and just generally horrible, and I stumbled across your content, and you're just so *good.* You reminded me that I'm perfect, just as I am. I use your recipes and workout suggestions, and I just *love* you."

Rhonda flings her arms around Sophie, and Soph hugs her right back, her eyes closed, rocking the other woman back and forth.

"You *are* beautiful," Sophie murmurs. "Just as you are, right now. And I'm so happy that I was there for you at a time of your life when you needed someone. You'll never know how much that means to me."

"God, I feel like a fool," Rhonda says as she wipes away tears. "But I just truly look up to you, and to have you just walk right into where I work, well, it's exciting and unexpected."

"I'm so happy to meet you," Sophie assures her.

God, I love her.

"Ike is also one of my favorite people," Rhonda confides as she looks over to me. "So, I think it's just awesome that the two of you are together."

"I think it's pretty awesome, too," Sophie says. "And I'm happy to be here, but I'm afraid that I'll just feel horrible for all the animals and want to take them all home with me."

"That's just part of the job," Rhonda replies. "My new partner, Jen, informed me that if I bring home any more animals, she'll move out. Not because she doesn't love me, but because there won't be any more room for her."

"Yeah, I can understand that," Soph replies. "Okay, what can I do to help?"

"You're with me today," I inform her. "I'll show you the ropes, and then next week, you can work on your own if you want."

"Awesome, lead the way."

"Before you go…" Rhonda turns to me with worried eyes. "Ike, I have bad news. Buster's back."

"What?" I scowl down at her and prop my hands on my hips. "He hasn't even been gone more than two weeks."

"He's a big dog, and the family just couldn't handle him. They didn't have patience for him, to be honest."

"You've *got* to be kidding me." My heart hurts for the Great Dane, who's been adopted and then brought back no less than four times.

"Who's Buster?" Sophie wants to know.

"The best dog ever," I reply immediately. "Come on, let's go say hi to the poor guy."

I take Sophie's hand in mine and lead her back to the dog kennels.

"Someone brought him back?" she asks. "That's horrible."

"And it's happened to him four times," I reply, my voice tight with anger. "He's a great dog, but he's *big*. He has good manners, and he just needs someone to be patient with him."

I approach the kennel, and when Buster sees me, his head comes up, and his tail starts to wag in excitement.

"Hey, buddy."

The dog jumps up to greet me, and when I unlock the kennel, he jumps up with his front feet on my shoulders and kisses my face.

"Yeah, I missed you, too. I'm sorry that you're back here in the slammer. We're going to find you a home. I promise, okay?"

His whole big body shakes with excitement as he turns circles, and then he approaches Sophie, who simply sits on the floor and kisses the dog's face.

Buster takes that as an invitation and lies down next to her, rests his head in her lap, and practically purrs with happiness.

"It's a good thing they brought him back," Sophie says between placing kisses on Buster's black head.

"Why's that?"

"Because he's yours." She turns those eyes up to me and grins. "He's clearly *your* dog, Ike. He adores you."

I cross my arms over my chest and grin. "I'm not the one he's all over right now."

"You didn't see his face when he realized you were here," she says, cuddling him. "You're his human. You're his safe person, Ike. You have to take him home."

"We talked about this. I can't take him. I can't stand the thought of boarding him when I'm out of town for games, and that would happen too much."

"Why? I can't take care of a dog?"

I pause and stare at her, not wanting to hope too hard.

"You're saying you'd take care of him when I'm gone?"

"Well, duh." Sophie kisses Buster's cheek. "We can manage without you for a day or two. Can't we, you big baby?"

Buster groans pathetically and rubs up against her, then smiles up at me with that big tongue hanging out of his mouth.

"I don't want to leave him here with the possibility that he'll never be adopted. He was here for more than a year when the last family took him."

"If you don't take him home, I will," Sophie says. "And I'd keep him at your house because you have the perfect yard for him."

I laugh now and then shrug. "Okay. You're coming home with me, buddy."

"That's just the sweetest thing I've ever heard." Rhonda is crying in the doorway, wiping her eyes furiously with tissues. "I just *knew* he belonged with you, but you're so stubborn."

"Luckily, the stubborn man has me now," Sophie says with a wink. "Can Buster follow us around while we work?"

"He should stay in here until we're ready to go," I reply. "Not all the cats are dog-friendly."

"Is Buster cat-friendly?"

We both look over at Rhonda, who nods. "Yes, we've tested him several times with cats and kids, and he's just the sweetest guy."

"Good to know." Sophie gives Buster one last kiss on the head before we put him back in the kennel long enough to do our chores.

"Don't tell me you want a cat, too."

"Maybe not today. But someday."

CHAPTER 15

SOPHIE

"So, your family owns an entire *vineyard*?"

"Yep." I grin over at Ike as he maneuvers through traffic on the freeway, heading toward Uncle Dominic's vineyard. "Dominic Salvatore has become quite accomplished in the wine industry over the years."

"Even *I* recognize that name, and I don't drink a lot of wine. Is he an uncle by marriage?"

I frown over at him. "No, why?"

"Because he doesn't use Montgomery as his last name."

"Ah." I nod and then let out a little laugh. "No, he doesn't. It's a sordid family story. A long, *long* time ago, when my uncle Caleb was just a toddler, my grandma and grandpa separated for a little while. During that time, my grandpa met an Italian woman and had an affair with her. Dominic was the result of that, but no one knew it for decades.

"Grandpa broke things off with Dom's mother to get back together with my grandma before anyone knew that the other woman was pregnant. And no one told him."

"Ouch," Ike says with a wince. "That's gotta hurt."

"I was alive when Uncle Dom came to find Grandpa, but I don't remember anything. I was little. Basically, his mom had passed away, and he was curious about his father. And, just as the Montgomerys always do with just about everyone, Dom was welcomed with open arms."

"Even by your grandma?"

"Especially by her," I reply with a nod. "I'm sure it hurt. It had to, right? But as far as I know, she's always been gracious and sweet to Dom. She always said that it isn't his fault. And she's right."

"Is this his only vineyard?" he asks as he changes lanes.

"No, he has one in Italy, as well, and I think he recently bought in as a partner down in California."

"That's pretty cool."

"Just wait until you see this place. It's *gorgeous.*"

Before long, we're pulling through the gates, and there are attendants to show us where to park.

"No paps," I say with surprise as Ike parks where directed. "I'm shocked."

"You said yourself that they arranged it this way to keep things under wraps."

"Yeah, but nothing is *ever* completely under wraps." I shake my head as he hurries around the truck, wearing an amazing tux that fits his tall body perfectly, and opens my door.

"Have I mentioned that you're absolutely stunning tonight?" He kisses my hand as I step onto the ground and grin up at him. Even in heels, he's far taller than me.

"Only twice."

"This dress." His eyes dance down over the burgundy dress I bought just last week when he was out of town. I'm relieved that it's not too cold outside because this little number has spaghetti straps, and the neckline falls down between my breasts, leaving no room for a bra.

My dad might have a heart attack.

The skirt is sheer, with velvet flowers that cover up all the important parts.

And with the strappy black heels, I'm feeling damn hot today.

"This dress," he says again, "should come with a warning label."

"Oh, I think it did. I must have forgotten to give it to you."

His lips tip up into a smug grin, and he leans in to whisper into my ear. "I can't wait to see it on the floor later."

"Can I keep the shoes on?"

He laughs now. "By all means, please do."

"Okay, enough flirting. Liv told me that she's mimicking Will and Meg's wedding. She wants the ceremony to be in the middle of the grape vines, with the reception up on the hill because of the amazing view."

"This place is something out of a magazine."

"Right? I told you it has a wow factor." I link my fingers with his, and we follow the others, making our way to where it looks like chairs are set up for the ceremony. "Not many chairs there."

I frown and look around, then flag down my aunt Alecia, Dom's wife and the organizer of this soiree.

"There aren't even fifty chairs out here," I say when she approaches.

"Sixty-five," she replies with a smile and then leans in to hug me. "And you're so dang beautiful, Sophie. This must be Ike."

She doesn't bother shaking his hand. She just hugs Ike as if she's known him forever.

"I've heard a lot about you."

"Same goes," Ike says. "It's nice to meet you."

"So, this shindig is smaller than I thought."

"Just close friends and family," Alecia confirms. "Liv didn't want anything huge. And so far, we're all clear on the media hounds."

"Good job on that."

"Thanks. We told everyone it was happening in

LA. I'm sure there are some confused paps down there today. I kind of love it. Anyway, I have to go check on dinner. I'll see you in just a bit." With that, she hurries off to make sure this event goes off without a hitch.

"Your family is all so friendly," Ike comments as we approach the chairs, probably half-full so far. "It's like none of them knows a stranger."

"They are," I agree. "They're good people. I mean, don't get me wrong, they can be scary if they're crossed or if someone we love is threatened. But all in all, you'll never meet a more inclusive bunch. Let's sit over there by my parents, if you don't mind."

"I don't mind, sweetheart."

God, I love it when he calls me sweetheart. With that slight hint of a southern drawl still hanging on to his voice, it's just so...*Ike.*

Mom waves us over and hugs me, then lets out a little wistful sigh. "Your dad is going to cover you up with his coat."

"No, I'm not," Dad replies, but he doesn't look happy as he leans in to kiss my cheek. "Really? Did you have to wear *this?*"

"There's nothing wrong with it," I reply simply.

"I think you left part of it at home," he grumbles, but then greets Ike, and that's all that's said on the matter.

"Dad's loosening up in his old age," I comment as I sit next to Mom.

"Who are you calling old, kiddo?" she asks, and we

both laugh. "I think it only took your father this long to realize that you're an adult and not a little girl."

"There's nothing about this dress that says *little girl.*"

"You're absolutely right about that," she says with a grin. "It's something your aunt Jules would have worn back in the day. Hell, she might still wear it, knowing her."

"I think *all* of you could pull this off."

"And that's why you're my favorite daughter."

"I'm your only daughter."

Before long, more people arrive, and the seats fill in. Our entire family is here, and we're not choosing sides, which is nice. We're spread out, talking and laughing and mingling with the other guests, making everyone feel welcome.

When I glance back and to the right, I almost swallow my tongue.

"Mom."

"Hmm?"

"I think Christian Wolfe is here with Jenna."

She frowns at me, shakes her head, and looks to where I indicate, and then she almost swallows *her* tongue. "Holy shit, I think you're right. Oh, it's so nice that they were able to make it. You know how close Christian is to both Luke *and* Vaughn."

"You know, I was raised with celebrities." I fidget with my dress and feel my face flush. "I don't get nervous around them very often. But he's always been my favorite."

"The star power at this wedding is impressive." Ike shifts in his seat as he turns back to me after chatting with my cousin, Hudson. "I just saw Jennifer Lopez walk in. And Leo Nash."

"Leo's my uncle," I inform him and watch as his eyes widen. "I know, it's a lot. I'll make you a family tree sometime."

The ushers make their way down the aisle with our grandparents, and soon, Aunt Natalie is escorted to her seat by my cousin, Keaton, who looks so handsome in his tux.

Keaton is never out of jeans and a T-shirt, so it's a treat to see him all dressed up.

And then, the music changes, and the bridal party walks down the aisle.

The bridal party is tiny. Liv just had Stella as her maid of honor, which totally makes sense because they're so close. And Vaughn asked Gray to be his best man.

Stella is just so pretty in her black slip dress, holding white flowers. I'm already getting teary-eyed.

The music changes again, and we all stand as Uncle Luke walks down the aisle with Liv on his arm.

"My God, there's never been a more beautiful bride."

I look back at Vaughn, whose eyes are shiny, and he has such a goofy look on his face; it just fills my heart with happiness.

If a man doesn't look at his bride like that, there's something wrong.

When I glance back to the bride and her daddy, they've stopped right in the middle of the aisle, and Luke frames her face with his hands. He leans in and kisses her forehead, and I can see him whisper, *I love you so much, baby girl.*

"Oh geez, Uncle Luke is the sweetest ever."

"Since the day he met Natalie," Mom confirms and wipes a tear off her cheek.

After a tender moment between father and daughter, Uncle Luke and Liv reach the front, and the officiate asks, "Who gives this woman to this man?"

"Her mother and I do," he replies, then kisses Olivia's cheeks. His eyes are full of tears when he offers Liv's hand to Vaughn, but before he can turn away, Vaughn pulls him in for a hug.

And we all sigh.

"You know, I've never really liked weddings," Ike says an hour later, as we eat salmon and drink truly excellent wine from Uncle Dom's cellars.

"Really? How come?"

"I think they're boring." He shrugs and munches on some broccoli. "They're always the same. But this one is definitely not boring."

"I'm glad." And he's right. There have been funny

223

toasts, a sweet first dance between the newly married couple, and Liv and her dad actually performed a choreographed number for the father-daughter dance.

It was awesome.

"There's not one helicopter overhead," I hear someone say. "How did they pull that off?"

Ike and I share a smile. "Between Uncle Luke, Leo, and all the others that have celebrity status in our family, they have a lot of practice in fooling the media."

"The press has been ramping up around me lately," Ike says with a frown. "I'm getting calls, people waiting outside the training center when I leave... There's always been a little of that, but they're getting more insistent."

"I would be shocked if they didn't do that, babe. You're hot news right now, with that new contract. Maybe things will mellow out again before the season starts in a couple of months."

"I hope so. I'm not a media hound. I just want to play ball."

"Part of the job," I remind him with a shrug. "You've got this."

"You have way more confidence than I do. Okay, let's change the subject to something way better. Wanna dance?" Ike sets his napkin aside and holds his hand out in invitation.

"I thought you hated to dance."

"It's a wedding." His smile is so damn sexy; how can

I resist him? I don't *want* to resist him. So, I place my hand in his and follow him out onto the floor.

It's a dreamy slow song. All the parents are coupled up and dancing, including my own parents, who are staring into each other's eyes.

"I used to hate it when they'd be all mushy in public," I say softly so only Ike can hear. "I thought it was so embarrassing."

"I think that's probably a normal reaction from kids."

"Hmm." I watch them for a few moments until Ike spins me away. "Now I'm grateful that they still look at each other like that. Like the other hung the moon. I'm not stupid. I know that they've had rough patches, but they always seem to work it out."

"You're lucky," he says. "I don't ever remember a time when my dad looked at my mom like that. When he was just flat-out *nice* to her, you know? I don't remember those days. Last week, when we were in Florida, I heard her laugh, like a big belly laugh, for the first time since I was a *kid.*"

"Wow." I brush my fingers through the back of his hair, wanting to soothe him. "That's really telling, Ike."

"So, it's different for me to be here, where everyone is happily married and enjoying themselves."

"Don't you think that a happy marriage is possible?"

"Yeah, I do." He nods and narrows his eyes like he's thinking it over. "I've just never witnessed one."

"Well, you will now."

Before he can reply, Keaton taps on Ike's shoulder and grins down at me.

"Just because you're dating her, doesn't mean you can monopolize all the dancing," Keaton says to Ike.

"I think that's *exactly* what it means," Ike says with a laugh. "But I'll share. I wanted to go chat with Will, anyway."

Ike kisses my cheek, and then Keaton spins me around the floor in a flourish. He always was an excellent dancer.

"You look good dressed up," I inform him. "You should do that more often."

"Right. Like I'm going to restore old cars in this getup. No thanks. You, however, look really nice tonight. I think all the uncles may have had a collective stroke."

"I'm not the only one showing some skin, you know."

"No, but you don't usually show so *much* skin."

I just shrug a shoulder, and then he twirls me around again, making me laugh.

"Do you know who she is?" he asks, gesturing to a woman who's talking to Uncle Leo and looks totally flustered doing it.

"That's Sidney, Gray's sister. She's a country singer. You've never heard her music? She's become really popular in the past couple of years."

"I'm not exactly a country fan," he says dryly. "I'm more of a Nirvana guy. But she's beautiful."

I look her way once more and smile softly. Sidney blushes as Leo talks to her. She's blonde with a gorgeous smile, and she's rocking that gold minidress like she was born to wear it. Clearly, the sexy genes run in the Sterling family. "Yeah, Sidney is gorgeous. And famous. You always said you'd stay away from anyone famous, Keat."

"No one said I was going to marry her. But I might just go say hi. There's no law against that."

"Is that the only reason you wanted to dance with me?" I scowl up at him. "You could have just gone and talked to her."

"If she's a Hollywood type, I'm not interested."

"She *is* famous."

"But she's not an actress." He winks at me. When the song is over, he quickly abandons me to go over to Sidney.

I've never spent any time with her myself. I only know who she is because Stella's told us all about her, and Sidney invited Stella and Olivia to a concert earlier this year. I hope that as Stella and Gray's wedding gets closer, I'll get to know her better, mostly because she just looks like she's really nice.

I walk to the edge of the dance floor and watch Keaton at work.

He smiles in that charming way he does, and when Sidney shakes his hand, he pulls it up to his lips so he can kiss her knuckles.

Yeah, he's laying it on thick.

But Sidney doesn't seem to mind. She laughs at something he says, and when he gestures and seems to ask a question, she nods enthusiastically.

Looks like Keaton might have just scored. Good for him.

"You're alone."

I look over in surprise to find my dad standing with me.

"Yeah. Ike's off talking football with Will, and Keaton just deserted me for a pretty girl."

"Sounds about right." He passes me a fresh glass of champagne. "How are things going with Ike?"

"We're doing well. He's a good guy, Dad."

He just nods and drinks his own champagne. "I like him. He looks at you like you're the best thing since football, and that's a good thing."

"He doesn't come from a great family. And I'm not talking financially or anything stupid like that. I mean, his dad isn't a good person."

Dad doesn't look surprised. "No, he isn't. I over-heard a phone conversation that night you introduced him to us. And then I did some digging there."

I stare at him in surprise. "*You* did some digging?"

"Our family has connections, Sophie. If you think I won't use them to keep you safe, you don't know me very well."

I let out a long breath. "Okay. What did you find out?"

"That his dad's an asshole. He isn't very nice to his

wife. Has some debt and likes to gamble. Nothing too crazy there, but he definitely spends beyond his means. He's not dangerous, and that was my main concern."

"I feel completely safe. And Ike got his mom out of there, moved her to Florida with her sister just last week."

"Good, I'm glad to hear that. What kind of security does Ike have at his house?"

I roll my eyes, but Dad just continues to look at me as if he's waiting for me to answer what I want for dinner.

"He has a gate and alarms on all the doors and windows."

"Okay." He nods and leans in to kiss my cheek. "Come on. Let's dance."

"You want to *dance*?"

He just raises an eyebrow, and I laugh. "Okay. Let's do it."

"MY DAD JUST ISN'T A DANCER," I say as I get out of the truck and wince at the pinching of my poor feet. The shoes were okay for the first couple of hours, and then they were basically torture devices. "Sure, he slow dances with my mom, but he spun me around that floor *three times*."

"You looked like you were having fun," Ike says with a grin and unlocks the door.

Buster comes running to greet us.

"Aww, hi sweet boy. Did you miss me?" I kiss his cheek three times and then rub his back vigorously. "You sweet man. I completely adore you."

"Is it possible to be jealous of a dog?" Ike winks at me as he takes off his jacket and tosses it over the back of a chair.

"He's just a baby. Aren't you, buddy?" I give Buster another kiss and then join Ike and give him a big hug. "You were awesome tonight. Thank you."

"I had a good time."

"I have to get out of this dress," I inform him. "And no, you don't have to rip it off of me. I want to get comfy and talk about all the things."

"You go ahead. I'll still get you naked later."

I smirk and walk up to his bedroom, where I have some clothes stashed. When I walk into the closet, I stop cold and take in the scene.

It looks like a massacre.

There are clothes and shoes all over the floor. My favorite running shoes have been chewed to a pulp.

"Ike?" I call out. "I need you to come in here."

"What's up?" I hear him jog up the stairs, and then he's behind me, and he lets out a long whistle. "Well, shit."

"I guess Buster didn't like being left alone. I told you we should have gated him in the kitchen or something."

"With what? A stern talking to?"

All I can do is shrug, and then we hear a little whine

come from behind us. We turn in unison to find Buster lying on the bed, looking completely pathetic.

"You're not innocent," I accuse the canine, pointing at him. "This is a bad thing. A bad, bad thing."

He just whines again and moves onto his back.

"Yeah, I can see that he's sorry." Ike takes a deep breath and lets it out slowly. "I think I'll have to call in a trainer for some help."

"Yeah. We might even have to get a ginormous crate for him. Or convert the guest room into his room or something."

"That's not a bad idea," Ike says, thinking it over. "We could even get some of that fake grass and put it in the corner so he can relieve himself if we're gone too long."

With that, we just stare at each other and then race through the house.

"I'll check the living room," I call out.

"I've got the game room," Ike replies.

We search and search, but don't find anywhere that Buster might have had an accident. But when I walk into the kitchen, I smell it.

"I think I found something," I call out, just as I hear Ike's phone buzz with an incoming text. "In the mudroom. How did we just walk right past this?"

Right there, in the middle of the room, is a pile of crap so big, it looks like it could have come from a horse.

Then again, Buster is *ginormous.*

I've just started to clean it up when Ike appears in the doorway, his face suddenly ashen.

"What's wrong? What is it?"

He shakes his head, then rubs his hand over his face in agitation.

I forget all about the dog poop and rush to him. "What's going on? Is your mom okay? Is she hurt?"

"It's not my mom," he finally says. "This is from my coach."

"Okay. What's going on?"

"They're accusing me of cheating."

CHAPTER 16

IKE

"*T*his is a bunch of fucking bullshit." I'm pacing Coach's office. I drove directly over here and met with Coach, the rest of the coaching staff, my attorney, and Will Montgomery, who came at Coach's request.

"You didn't have to leave Liv's wedding for this," I say to my mentor, but he just shakes his head.

"I'd just gotten home when I got the text. I wouldn't be anywhere else."

"What in the hell is even going on?" I demand. "We didn't *win* the championship game. Not to mention, I've never cheated at anything a day in my life."

"Someone said something to the press," Coach says. He looks tired and stressed. "They're calling it a *reliable source*, although they won't name names, so it's probably just bullshit."

"It's credible enough that we're all sitting here, in

this room, waiting for Florence and her people to get here so we can have a big meeting about it at freaking two in the morning," Sal, my offensive line coach, says. "So it's not a prank."

"There will probably be an investigation," my attorney, Alex, says. "Ike could be suspended during the time the investigation is underway."

"How long does that take?" I demand.

"Could be a few weeks, could be a year."

"A *year*? A fucking *year*? No way. I didn't do anything wrong. I didn't deflate balls or whatever it is that they're saying."

"There are a few allegations," Alex continues. "One is that you've come into possession of the San Francisco playbook and have been in cahoots with Coach."

I snort at that one. "I don't give a *fuck* about their playbook."

"Another," Alex says, ignoring my outburst, "is that you use Stickum or Gorilla Glue on your towel to have better control of the ball."

I shake my head, staring at the other man. "Have you seen the size of my hands? I don't need glue. I have long fingers. Jesus."

"And finally, that you're on a controlled and performance-enhancing drug."

"Steroids?" I stare at him like he's lost his ever-loving mind. "I work my fucking *ass off*, Alex. I train twice a day. My girlfriend makes me the grossest green smoothies for breakfast that I *hate*, but she says are good for me, so I pretend that I like them, and I drink them anyway. If you want her recipe, I'm sure she'll be happy to give it to you."

"They very well may want that, yes."

"Jesus, Alex," Will says with a sigh. "This isn't the first time someone has been accused of something like this. Hell, people *do* shit like this. Remember when Buffalo used to open their stadium doors to create the wind tunnel onto their field to throw off the visiting team? That shit was *cold* and found to be illegal by the league."

"Listen, the worst that's going to happen is you'll get fined and maybe miss a game or two." Sal shoves his hands into his pockets and rocks back on his heels. "The league may try to scare us all, but at the end of the day, it's just a slap on the wrist."

"I'm not missing a game for this," I interject. "I didn't do anything wrong. Test me for Christ's sake. You'll see that I don't have any drugs in my body."

"Boys."

We all turn to find Florence standing in the door-way, a smug smile on her old face.

Her gaze flicks over Will in disdain and then lands on me.

"You know, I just *knew* that you'd turn out to be a disappointment. Meet us in the conference room in fifteen minutes so we can decide how in the hell we're going to spin this to our benefit."

She stomps away, and her assistant, Brandon,

pauses in the doorway. He looks like he wants to say something. His jaw is clenched.

But then Florence snaps out, "Jesus, Brandon, get over here," and he hurries off.

"He knows something," I say, pointing at the doorway.

"He only knows what Florence wants him to know," Coach says. "He's an errand boy, nothing more."

"Okay." Coach blows out a breath and runs his big, beefy hand down his hang-dog face. "Let's get this meeting over with. Ike's already said that he'll comply with drug testing. We can prove that we don't have glue anywhere in the facility."

"What about the playbook?" Sal asks.

"Doesn't exist," Coach replies simply. "Let's go."

I'M surprised to find Sophie sitting on the couch with Buster snoring away at her feet when I get home around five in the morning.

There's a single lamp illuminating her as she's curled up with a book in her hands, and she looks up to watch me walk into the room.

"How was it?"

"Pretty shitty." I sit next to her and lean my head back on the cushions. "We'll be denying everything and cooperating with the league to provide proof for all the allegations. I hate Florence. That bitch has no business owning this team. I'm telling you, I think she *wants* us to lose."

"Why do you think that?"

"Because she tried to push for me to sit out the first four games of the season."

"Why would you do that?"

"Good question. She said it would show good faith, but the entire team, including all of her own attorneys, said it would only show that I was guilty and that I had something to be ashamed of. She balked at that."

"She's stupid," Sophie says, shaking her head. "Your backup quarterback is a rookie, right?"

"Yeah, and he's a nice guy, but he's green and has a lot to learn. He's not ready to start. If I sit out, we have the possibility of losing all those games, and then our position in the playoffs could be in jeopardy from the start."

"She just doesn't know what she's doing," Soph replies softly. "Ike, anyone who knows you *knows* that you didn't do anything you're being accused of."

"That doesn't matter." I'm so exhausted that I'm surprised I can stand, but I do and pace to the windows. It's so dark out that I can't see the water, but I stare out into the blackness anyway. "What matters is that the press is going to sink their teeth into this and run with it. Fans will talk, and sales could be hurt. Seattle fans are *rabid*. I could walk out for that first game to nothing but boos."

"You won't," she says, but I shake my head.

"If I had done any of the things I'm accused of, I would be upset, but I would take it on the chin. I fucked up, and these are the consequences. But I didn't do those things, Soph. And you know, shit like this has always happened."

"You've been accused of cheating before?"

"No, just *shit*. I feel like when I get ahead, something happens to knock me down a peg. It's usually my old man pulling this shit on me, so I can't actually *enjoy* anything that I've worked hard for."

I stop speaking, and a niggling idea sets up residence in the back of my head. When I turn to Sophie, she's watching me with wide blue eyes, and I can see that she's thinking the same thing.

"Ike, you don't think—"

"No." I shake my head and pace the room. "Don't even say it. He wouldn't do this."

"You know him," she says simply. "And you know that he *would*."

I blow out a breath and shake my head again. "I know he's mad. Maybe even hurt, because I really do think that he believes, down to the marrow of his bones, that I owe him everything, and now he's wallowing in self-pity. But this? No. I refuse to believe it."

"I know you don't want to think that your own father could do something like this, but don't discount it," she advises. "You're too smart, Ike. Set your emotions aside and think about this. Is he capable of it?"

I just stare back at her, and I know, down in my gut, the answer to that question.

Hell, yes, he's capable of it.

I sit next to her again and drop my head in my hands. "He's my *dad.*"

"I know." She scoots over and wraps her arms around me, tugs me into her, and holds on tight. "I'm so sorry, babe."

"I need to sleep, even if it's for a couple of hours. I have to be back at the training center at nine for a press conference."

"That's in *four hours.*"

"Yeah. Come on." I pull her to her feet and lead her upstairs to the bedroom. Buster follows, but he must know that I just need to be with my girl tonight because he curls up on his big, new bed in the corner of the room and goes back to sleep.

After we've stripped out of our clothes, we slip under the covers, and I pull her to me.

I want to make love to her. I want to lose myself in her and forget all about this whole bullshit situation.

But for now, I need to just hold her.

And because Sophie knows me so damn well, she curls up against me and buries her face in my neck.

"I love you," she whispers under my ear. "And I'm with you all the way."

"I love you, too." I tighten my hold on her. "Thank you."

Knowing that she's on my side is *everything.*

She's all I need.

~

"Have you called your dad?" Sophie asks two days later. Two hellish days of medical appointments and being interrogated by investigators, and that's all on top of the endless interviews and press conferences.

People want to discuss it into the ground, over and over again, and all I can say is *no comment,* and *I didn't do that.*

I'm sick of hearing the sound of my own voice.

"No," I reply as I set the glass from the green smoothie she made me into the dishwasher. "And I won't be."

"Personally, I think you should confront him, Ike."

"Thanks for your opinion."

Yeah, I sound like a dick. I don't fucking care. I'm so *tired* of all of this, and we're still at the beginning.

"Hey, I'm not trying to be a nag, I just think—"

"I love you," I interrupt her and turn to take her shoulders in my hands. "More than anything. Hell, I love you *more* than football, sweetheart, but I don't want to talk about this, okay? I need a break."

"Okay." She offers me a small smile. "Sorry. I know

it's been a rough few days. Let's take the afternoon off from all of it. No work talk."

"Yes, please. What do you have in mind?"

"Let's hop on a ferry over to the best island there is, have lunch at an awesome Irish pub that just happens to be in the family, by marriage, and then we can come back here, or my place, and have marathon sex."

"Wow. That sounds like the best day ever."

"*And* we have to turn off our phones. We'll take them with us, just in case of an emergency."

"Even better." I lean in and kiss her. "Let's put this plan into action *immediately.*"

"What about Buster?"

We both look over at the big dog, who's been watching and *listening.* He's a smart dog.

"Actually," Sophie says, thinking it over. "I bet my cousins would enjoy having him over at the compound. There's always someone home, and he'll have another great yard to play in."

"Do you think they'd be okay with that? That's a big imposition."

Sophie just shakes her head and reaches for her phone. "Nah. I'll text Liam and see if someone is game."

She is quiet as she taps on the screen, and then she grins.

"Liam and Hudson are home and said to bring him over."

"Let's go."

It's been rainy today, so we grab jackets and scarves for the ferry, and we're off. We drop off Buster at the compound, and he doesn't even look back at us as he's welcomed inside with lots of pats and excitement. Then, it's a good drive into the city to catch the ferry, but before long, we're loaded up onto the ferry, my truck safely parked below, and I'm on the deck with Soph tucked under my arm, watching the city fade into the distance.

"I needed this today," I say softly. "And I'm sorry that I've been a dick a lot over the past couple of days."

"You're not a dick; you're frustrated," she replies. "Trust me, I'm not a pushover. If I thought you were acting like a complete ass, I'd call you out on it."

"Good." I kiss the top of her head and breathe her in. "Tell me about this pub and the island."

"Okay, this could require more spreadsheets." She laughs in that sweet way that makes me feel warm inside. "I have a cousin named Anastasia. She's actually a second cousin of mine, a first cousin to my dad."

"So far, I'm following."

"She married Kane O'Callaghan, the glass artist."

"The one with a whole freaking museum dedicated to his work here in Seattle?"

"That's the one." Her smile is brilliant. "I take it you've heard of him."

"I think most people have heard of him. Okay, so you're related to Kane O'Callaghan."

"I am, by marriage. And his family, which is also a big one, lives on this island. They own O'Callaghan's

Pub and are *very* Irish. Some of the O'Callaghan siblings work there, in the pub, and some do other things, but pretty much all of them still live and work out here on the island."

"That's pretty cool."

We're quiet for a while, and then she snaps her head up and stares at me with horror.

"Oh, shit."

"What is it?"

"Damn, I forgot to tell you something. Don't get mad, okay?"

"I can't promise that. Just tell me what's up."

"Well, damn it." She bites her lip, winces, and then continues. "So, my grandma and grandpa want to have everyone over to their house this Saturday for the first barbecue of the season, and I told them that we'd be there, but I didn't even check with you. I completely forgot. If you'd rather not go, I can go alone. It's not a big deal."

I like Sophie's family, but I've never seen a family that gets together so damn much. It seems to be *constant.*

Yeah, I'd like a little break to catch my breath. The wedding was less than a week ago.

But I can see the hope in her eyes, and I'll be damned if I turn her down.

"It's fine. We'll go."

"Are you sure?"

"I'm sure."

"If you change your mind, just say so, okay?"

"I will tell you if I change my mind, but I don't think I will."

The ferry docks, and we return to where the truck is parked so I can drive it off the boat and onto the island, which is really beautiful.

"I love it out here," Sophie says with a happy sigh. "Like, *really* love it. I used to think that I'd move out here since I can work from anywhere."

"Now you don't want to?"

"It's not convenient," she replies. "It's a commute to the city from here, and I like the convenience of being close to everything in Seattle, including the family. But I really do love it here."

"You could always have a vacation house here," I reply, thinking it over as I drive through the small village. "Come on the weekends or for a week here or there."

"Oh, that's not a bad idea." I can see the wheels turning in her head, and then she points to the left. "There it is. O'Callaghan's."

"I see it." I find parking, and then take her hand and lead her to the door of the pub, then pull it open.

When we step inside, it's like we've been transported to Ireland. Irish music plays through the speakers, and it's exactly what I would expect a pub in Ireland to look like.

"Wow."

"I know, right?" She laughs and waves to a man behind the bar. "Hey, Keegan!"

"Well, Sophie, me love. It's been too long since I last laid me eyes on ye." Keegan rushes around the bar and scoops Sophie into a hug and then turns to me with a friendly smile and his hand to shake. "I'm Keegan, the owner of this fine pub. You must be Sophie's man."

"I am. Ike Harrison."

"Ike—" Keegan breaks off, the smile leaves his face, and then he stares at Sophie before turning back to me. "Well, that's the way of it, then? I'm a big fan, Ike."

"Thanks."

"Come on and sit at the bar so we can have a chat."

"I have a question for you, Keegan," Sophie says as she takes her stool. "Does Maeve still sell real estate here on the island?"

"Aye, my sister does, yes. Are you thinking of moving over here, then?"

She glances at me with twinkling eyes and then back at Keegan.

"I don't know. I'm just kicking around some ideas."

Hell, if she wants a place here, she'll have it. I'll gladly buy it for her. We could easily sell her condo and buy a place here but live full time in my house.

Yeah, it's a hell of a good idea.

"Would you like a Guinness, Ike? On me, of course."

"You know, I've never had one," I reply. "But I'm driving."

"Let's share one," Sophie suggests. "And we'll get food to soak it all up."

"Shawn's in the kitchen today," Keegan says with a smile as he grabs a glass and begins to pull the taps. "I'll call him out to say hi and take your order."

"Is your father here?" Sophie asks him, and I see Keegan's face immediately fall.

Oh no.

"He's been a bit under the weather. He's staying with Maeve these days, enjoying the view of the ocean and tending to her garden."

"I always loved your parents," Sophie says softly.

"Me, too." Keegan winks at her and then yells back to a set of double doors. "Shawn, get your arse out here, will ye?"

The doors open, and a man, just as tall as Keegan, comes walking out of the kitchen and smiles when he sees Sophie.

"Hello, darling." Shawn is more soft-spoken than his brother. "It's good to see you."

"You, too. Will you make me a burger? And do you have your famous stew?"

"For you, anything."

CHAPTER 17

"*Y*esterday was fun." Ike's face is still sleepy as he turns to me in the early morning light. "I learned things about you that I didn't expect."

"Such as?" I turn on my side and brace my head on my hand, leaning on my elbow and smiling down at him.

"You want a house on an island."

"Yeah, but I'm kind of picky with that." I narrow my eyes at him. "I want an ocean view. Doesn't have to be ocean*front*, but I want the view."

"What else?" He snuggles under the covers, and I can just see his face. "What else do you want, sweetheart?"

"That's the biggest thing, I guess." I bite my lip, thinking it over. "It doesn't have to be a big house. I just need space for an office, and it should have lots of light for when I'm filming."

"Got it."

"Are you making a mental list?"

"Maybe." He grins and reaches out for me. "You're too far away. Come here."

Happily, I fall into Ike's arms, and when his hands roam down my naked sides to my ass, I crawl over him until I'm straddling his hips and smiling down at him.

"I know this is going to sound shallow," he begins and cups my breasts in his hands. "But you have magnificent tits."

I giggle and then moan as I slide back and forth over his already hard length. God, I love the way he feels against me. And his hands cupping my breasts is just the icing on the cake.

There's no more conversation as our bodies fall into a familiar rhythm, moving together in a dance so simple, so elemental, that it shocks me at how much it draws us closer together.

But before I can take him inside of me, he reverses our positions and kisses me, nibbling at my lips and whispering that he needs me.

He lifts one of my legs and slips right inside, making me gasp.

"Jesus, Ike."

"Just Ike," he says, but I don't laugh.

I can't do anything except be swept away by what his body does to mine.

"Grab on to that pillow, babe."

I immediately do as I'm told. I don't have my wits about me yet to try to work under my own brain-power, so with my hands over my head, Ike's hands roam again. His mouth fastens onto my breast, and I'm just a ball of sensation, loving every second of him.

Finally, his mouth works its way up to my ear. "I can't get enough of you. I *crave* you every minute of every fucking day, Sophie."

"Same." My voice, so breathless and thin, surprises me. "Never enough. Jesus Christ."

"Either you've recently become *really* religious, or you just really like what I'm doing to you."

"That last one." I have to swallow hard. I feel the orgasm working its way down my spine and up my thighs. "Gonna come. Oh, fuck me, I'm gonna come."

"Do it." He bites my neck, and that's all it takes to send me over the edge, crying out in ecstasy as my body pulses with wave after wave of pure sensation, my pussy milking his cock until he, too, succumbs to his own climax, growling against my neck.

"That's a *really* great way to start the day," I murmur.

"Nothing better," he agrees. "There is absolutely *nothing* better than this."

"That's high praise, coming from someone like you. Can I put my arms down now? I think they're going numb."

He laughs and moves my arms, kissing each one as he does.

"You're good at taking orders."

"Only in bed, so don't go getting any ideas, buddy."

That makes him laugh even more, and a small knot that I didn't even realize I had loosens in my belly.

"It's good to hear you laugh again."

"I haven't been very much fun lately."

"Look." I sit up and push my hair out of my face. "It's never going to be all laughs and good times, every single day. Never. There will be work stress, family stress, health stress, or *something.* I don't expect you to always act like the whole world is carefree."

"I know."

"What's happening next with the investigation?" I need to ask him because he's not very forthcoming with information. I don't think he's trying to shut me out; he's just used to internalizing everything, so I have to prod it out of him.

"Now, I guess we wait and see what they find. I've done my part by giving all the blood samples and information."

"That's all you can do." I lean over and kiss his lips lightly, and I can hear someone out in my kitchen. "Oh, I think Becs is here."

Just then, Becs herself walks right through the bedroom door. "Soph? I'm here—oh. Oh, shit. My eyes."

She covers her eyes and runs out of the room, and I

stare down at the two of us, stark naked, out of the covers, and it's clear as day what we just finished doing.

"Well. I guess Becs knows me on a whole new level now."

"Me, too," Ike says with a shrug. "Ah, well. I guess that's my cue to get up and go get Buster. Do you have a full day?"

"Pretty full. But, the more we get done today, the less I have on my plate through the weekend, which is good since we have the barbecue at my grandparents' house tomorrow."

"Right."

He doesn't sound ecstatic. "If you don't want to go, I really won't be hurt over it."

"I do want to go." He leans in to kiss my cheek. "I do. I'm going to pull on some clothes in case Becs walks back in here and I ruin her for all other men in her life."

I smirk. "You're so modest."

"It's a bunch of bullshit, that's what it is," my uncle Matt says, shaking his head as we chat with him and Nate, Stella's dad, at the barbecue the next day. "That some random asshole can just accuse you out of the blue and ignite a whole investigation is just bullshit."

I glance up at Ike and see that he just politely nods. I *know* he's sick of talking about this.

"We haven't met."

I turn and see Uncle Caleb, the former Navy SEAL and the toughest one in the family, standing behind us. His steely gaze is on Ike.

"Ike Harrison." He holds out his hand to shake, but Caleb just stares at it. "Uh, nice to meet you."

"Give me one good reason why I shouldn't punch you in the face."

"Uncle Caleb, it's okay. Ike's actually a nice guy."

"I don't give a shit. He's trying to date my niece."

"Do you punch every guy who tries to date a girl in this family?" Ike asks.

Caleb just narrows his eyes at him.

"Seriously, this is completely ridiculous." I roll my eyes. "Uncle Caleb isn't going to punch you."

"Looks like he might."

"He won't," Matt replies and slaps Caleb on the back good-naturedly. "He just likes to act scary. Come on, let's get some ribs before Will eats them all."

The other men leave, and Ike takes a deep breath.

"Sorry. Caleb is really just a softy."

"Yeah, looks like he is," Ike says, and his jaw clenches as he looks over the backyard.

"You don't want to be here, do you." It's not a question.

"It's fine."

"Don't lie to me."

"Fine." His voice is low so only I can hear. "Your

family *is* a lot. You spend more time together than I ever knew was even a *thing.*"

"We're a close family."

"And that's great. But I'm not used to it. And I'm damn sick of talking about all the shit going down at work."

"I know." I cringe. "They're just trying to show you that they support you."

He blows out a breath and nods. "You're right. I know you're right. And I appreciate it."

He's not trying to keep me from them; he's just not used to them. He said himself that he doesn't even remember a time in his life when his dad was kind to his mom.

That's a far cry away from my own family.

"Listen, we can duck out early. It's totally fine."

"No. No, I'm sorry. It's fine."

But, before I can even blink, my parents walk over to us, and my mom wraps Ike up into a big hug.

"I'm so sorry for what you're going through, honey," she says, and Ike's expression hardens all over again.

Damn it.

"He'll be fine," Dad says to her and watches my face. His eyes narrow.

I give him a slight shake of the head.

It's okay.

"We went to the island the other day," I say, trying to change the subject. "We saw some of the

253

O'Callaghans and had some good food, then looked around over there."

"Oh, the island is gorgeous," Mom says and nods. "We love it over there, too. What did you think of it, Ike?"

"It's really special," he says, already relaxed, and that makes me feel better. I want him to feel at ease with my family. "There are some really crazy views from out there, and the pub was fun. They seem like a nice bunch."

For a while, it seems like a crisis was averted. Conversation veers all over the place, from the island to investments, to *basketball*, which is fun to talk about rather than football.

Natalie tells us all that Liv and Vaughn are having a great honeymoon in the Maldives, and she shares some photos with us.

"Wow, it's really pretty there," I comment, looking over Natalie's shoulder. "The magazines definitely aren't photoshopped."

"I vote for the Maldives *next* Christmas," Stella calls out, holding her glass of iced tea up high. "We did snow in Iceland last year. Let's do tropical this year!"

"You guys went to Iceland for Christmas?" Ike asks, looking shocked.

"Yeah, the whole family went," I reply. "It's the first, and probably the last, time we did something like that. We're all too busy to make it happen."

Ike's phone buzzes in his pocket, and he pulls it out, frowning down at it.

But he doesn't answer it.

"Everything okay?" Dad asks him.

Ike just nods. "Yeah, it's fine."

But it's *not* fine.

The phone buzzes again, and this time Ike doesn't even look down at it.

"Is it your dad?" My voice is soft, but the others next to us can hear me.

"I'll talk to him later," Ike says.

"You're welcome to go inside and take it in private," Dad offers. "It's not a problem."

"It's okay," Ike says. "I'm sure it can wait until later."

"What if something's wrong?" Nat asks. "Maybe he needs you. You should really just go and call him."

"It's *fine*," Ike says again, his voice tight now, and he steps away, walking into my grandpa's garden.

"I put my foot in it," Natalie mutters.

"It's okay. It's been a really shitty week." I pat her arm and then take off after my boyfriend. "Hey."

"Look, you were probably right all along. I should have bowed out. I just didn't want to disappoint you, but it wasn't a good idea that I came. I'm not trying to be rude."

"I'm not upset." And it's the truth. I'm not. "You're dealing with a lot of stuff, Ike. I probably wouldn't want to hang out with a bunch of strangers, either."

"They're nice. But man, are they *always* in your business like this?"

Okay, now I might get upset.

"If *in my business*, you mean do we get together often? Yes. Do they keep up with each of us and the things happening in our lives? Absolutely. I see my cousins several times a month and the parents once a month. More in the summer."

"I don't know how to do that." He's looking down at his sneakers, his hands on his hips. "I don't know what that looks like, Soph, and I'm not so sure that I can deal with it. It sounds great, but I don't know if it's something that I can have. Hell, I don't think it's something I *deserve*."

"What are you even talking about?"

He shakes his head, refusing to look at me. "We're so different. You deserve someone who fits in during things like this."

"You *do* fit in."

"You need someone who doesn't mind getting the third degree whenever he spends time with your family."

Now I don't know what to say. What in the hell is happening?

"So, let me get this straight." I don't even bother to keep my voice down now. "You're bailing on me because I have a wonderful family? What kind of absolute bullshit is that, Isaiah Harrison?"

Now he does look at me, and the hurt I see in his eyes is enough to break me.

"Ike."

"No." He shakes his head once and scratches his chin. "You're right. I'm fucked-up. This whole thing is fucked-up. I'd better go before we say more shit we don't mean, and I make even more of an ass out of myself."

He walks through the crowd that's now watching us and listening intently, then through the gate, letting it swing closed behind him.

"You have *got* to be kidding me," I mutter in frustration. "Who bails because their girlfriend's family is *too* nice? Like, who even does that?"

I move to set off after him, but Will puts his hand on my shoulder.

"Hang on, tiger. Let me have a word with him. I would tell you to calm down, but that usually puts me in the doghouse for a few days."

"Yeah, don't tell her that," Meg suggests as Will walks out the gate after Ike.

"I won't feel like I have to walk on eggshells around *anyone.* Not ever."

"And you shouldn't," Grandma Gail says with a soft smile. "But that boy isn't trying to hurt you or us. I saw it the minute you two arrived. He's grieving."

"*Grieving?*" I stare at her. "I don't—oh. His dad."

My own father nods. "We can all piece together

257

who said something to the media about Ike cheating, honey. Even Ike sees it."

"He won't call his dad out on it," I reply, looking over at the gate.

"And then we didn't stop talking about it," Mom says. "That wasn't good."

"No, none of us should feel like we have to sidestep him," I reply.

"Of course not," Grandma says. "But we *should* be mindful of how he's feeling. I think he's a good young man who has a full plate right now. It's good that Will is talking to him."

"I'm going out there, too," I decide and walk toward the fence. I can't stand to see Ike hurting.

I need to fix it.

CHAPTER 18

IKE

"*W*ait up."

I stop at the truck and look back to see Will jogging toward me.

"I'm sorry," I begin. "I shouldn't have spoken to her that way, definitely not in front of the whole family, but also not at all. I'm just not myself right now, and I shouldn't have come. I'm not sure that she should be with me at all, Will."

"Okay, hold on." Will leans on the truck and crosses his arms over his chest. "I don't want to have to cut out your heart and eat it. That's just not appetizing to me."

"Fuck, is she *crying*?"

"No, she's mad as hell."

I feel my lips twitch. "It's hot when she's mad."

"You love her."

"More than anything. That's why I'm here today."

"But you don't like her family?"

Ashamed, I shake my head. "No. That's not it at all. Everyone's been great. I have no reason to dislike anyone in there. But it's a *lot*, Will. I have three other members in my family. Well, my sister is married and has two kids, so add them in, but that's it, and none of them lives anywhere near me. My sister couldn't get out of the house soon enough after she graduated, and I couldn't blame her. I haven't seen her in two years."

"I'm sorry to hear that."

"I'm not saying any of this to get sympathy; I'm just trying to explain where I'm coming from."

"I get that." Will nods slowly, then looks back at his parents' house. "My parents moved in here when Caleb was little—just before I was born, I think. Lived here all my life. I'm not the one that paid it off for them. It wasn't Jules or any of the other brothers."

I frown at him, listening.

"It was Natalie. She came into the family when she was in college with Jules. They were best friends, and Natalie lost her parents in a plane crash. She inherited some money, not that any of us was concerned about that. My parents just wanted to give her a place to land, you know?"

I nod, but I don't know what that's like at all.

"She was the first one that we brought into the family that didn't necessarily belong here by blood. After college, her business was taking off, so she paid off my parents' house because she was grateful to them and because she loves them."

Will sighs and looks back over to me.

"I had offered to pay off their mortgage many times before that. My parents were *not* broke, but like most families, they had a mortgage to pay. They wouldn't let me. My dad told me that the money I made from playing was *my* paycheck, not his. Every time I offered, they'd thank me, and Dad would say, '*Nah, I'm fine, son.*'"

"But they let Natalie?"

"They didn't have a choice. She didn't ask. She simply *did.* That's pretty typical for the women in our family. She called up the bank and paid for it. And I wasn't mad. It ended up happening that way for a reason, I guess. Natalie felt that she needed to do it for my parents. She wanted to repay them for their love and hospitality. I guess I'm telling you this because you've been beating yourself up for giving all that money to your dad."

"It was way more than just paying off a mortgage."

"I know that. And I know that you did it for different reasons, too, but you weren't wrong for doing it. No matter how bad your dad can be, you still love him, and you wanted to help him *and* your mom because they're your parents."

"Yeah, and look where it got me. I stood up to him, and he fucking spewed lies about me and tried to ruin my career."

Will's eyes narrow on me. "Do you know that for sure?"

"I've done the math, Will. I don't have to confront him. He'd lie about it anyway."

My phone rings again, which just pisses me off more.

"All I wanted in life was for my dad to be proud of me. That's it. But not one time did he ever say those words to me. All he did was bask in what he considered *his* glory and hold his hand out. This last contract? He called it *ours.*"

I shake my head and pace down the length of the truck and back again.

"And now, I have this whole shit show going on with the team because he's pissed off, even after everything I fucking did for him."

My phone rings again.

"You should answer that."

I stare down at my dad's name and then hit accept.

"Yeah."

He's quiet for a second. "Hi, Ike. Listen, I'm not thrilled to be making this call. I don't have much to say to you right now."

"Then I guess I can hang up."

"Wait. Don't do that." I can just picture him scowling. "You should know that I got a call about a week ago from Florence. She was going to offer to pay me a lot of money to call the media and tell some lies about you. Now, I admit, I was pretty pissed about everything, and I still am, but I told her no."

"Why are you calling me *now*? Why didn't you call

me when it happened?"

"Because you're on my shit list, son." His voice is loud and defiant, and I wipe my hand over my mouth in agitation.

"Easy," Will says.

"But I think you should know who you're working for."

"How do I know this isn't another lie? A game?"

"I'm not lying to you. Believe what you want, but I said what I needed to. Good luck."

He hangs up, and I just stare at the phone.

"I don't know if I can believe him."

"I do."

My head whips up at Will's comment. "Why?"

"What does he have to lose? He's not lying. And, knowing Florence, it doesn't surprise me that she'd pull something like this."

Before I can ask more questions, my phone rings again, and Will's phone pings with a message.

"We're popular today," I mutter and answer the phone, putting it on speaker. "This is Ike."

"This is Alex," my attorney says. "There's been a development. It seems that Florence didn't take into consideration that when you were accused of cheating, the entire team would be put under a microscope."

Will and I look at each other in surprise.

"Okay. What's happened?"

"Turns out, Florence has been betting *against* the team for quite some time. You weren't cheating, *she* was. She's the reason you lost the championship. She rigged everything. Paid off people."

"Motherfucker."

"Certainly," Alex agrees. "She's in deep shit. It's likely the league will make her sell the team. She won't recover from this."

"What happens in the meantime?"

"Administratively, things get crazy, but for you, not much will change. I expect there will be a formal, public apology to you. I'll be in touch as I know more."

"Thanks, Alex."

I hang up and stare at Will.

"That's why she tried so hard to get you to not sign that contract," Will says. "Why she had ridiculous clauses included. So you'd walk. She never wanted to win."

"And it really wasn't my dad."

Suddenly, arms encircle my waist from behind, and I feel Sophie rest her face on my back.

"Congratulations," Will says with a smile. "I'll leave you two to it."

Pulling Sophie around so I can face her, I take her face in my hands and rest my forehead on hers.

"I'm so sorry, sweetheart."

"I hate to see you hurting," she says softly. "I'm not mad, Ike. No one is. I'm just worried about you. And if you think you can dump me just because I have the best family in the world, you're an idiot."

That makes me smile. "It wasn't my dad."

"I heard. And I'm so relieved."

"Me, too. I mean, I don't want a relationship with him, and I'm still not giving him any money, but it's a relief to know that he didn't try to ruin me out of spite. It was eating me alive."

"I heard that Florence is on the outs, too."

"Yeah. The whole mess is coming to a close."

Sophie hugs me tightly and kisses my cheek. "I need you to know something really important."

"Okay, I'm listening."

"I love you. But I also love my family. I know they're big and loud, and they're in my business, but I *love* them. I can't and won't see less of them or cast them off for anyone in the world, not even for you."

"I know that, and I would *never* ask you to. I'm not the guy who would try to alienate you from the people who love you."

"I don't believe you are. If I did, we wouldn't be having this conversation. I also can't feel like I'm walking on eggshells whenever we're around them, worried that you're uncomfortable."

"I'll apologize to you now, and I'll go back there and do the same. I'm so sorry for the way I acted. I can usually take a lot of pressure. I work *best* under pressure. But all this really took a toll on me. I didn't want to discuss it with *anyone*, especially not the people that I'm trying to make a good impression on. Although I kind of fucked all of that up on my own."

"Nah, they're pretty understanding. Grandma

reminded us all that you've been grieving."

Unable to reply, I just push her hair off of her shoulder. "Your grandma's pretty smart."

"Smarter than me," she says, and now she has tears in her eyes. "I'm sorry that I didn't realize it, Ike. I knew you were angry, and maybe even a little scared, but I didn't take into consideration the sadness you must feel about your dad. About the whole situation. And then to just parade my functional family under your nose is just rude."

"So rude." I laugh when her eyes grow wide. "I'm kidding. I don't want you to be anything other than what you are. You're amazing. And I'll eventually get used to having a big, nosy family poking around."

"So, I'm not single again."

My heart stutters at the idea. "Honey, you're *never* going to be single again"

When we return to the backyard, no one stops and stares. No one tries to run over and take me out. Everyone's just doing their thing, laughing and talking.

But then Liam comes jogging over and claps his hand on my shoulder. "I guess you don't have to die today. Uncle Caleb looked a little murderous for a minute, but then we decided that burying a body is a pain in the ass and made the decision to let you live."

"I appreciate it." I clear my throat. "Hey, everyone."

I wait while the family turns to me, and I've never been so fucking nervous in my life.

"I just want to apologize to you all for the way I

acted earlier. I've had a really rough week, and I guess it all overwhelmed me today, but that's no excuse. Sophie is way too important to me to ever embarrass her or treat her badly. It won't happen again."

"Oh, so you're human." Stacy grins at me. "You don't have to apologize for that, Ike."

And, just like that, they all go back to what they were doing, and the matter is seemingly over.

They just forgave me, without asking me to grovel or expecting something from me.

Yeah, Sophie has the best family I've ever met. And for whatever reason, they've included me, as if I've been here all along.

I won't be fucking that up again.

"I DON'T WANT or need this press conference," I mutter to Sophie and sigh as she adjusts my tie.

"You may not want it, but it's definitely needed. You deserve a public apology after all the shit they put you through."

I shake my head, but I don't argue. I just want things to get back to normal when it comes to work.

With Sophie by my side, her hand clasped firmly in my own, we walk out from behind a curtain covered with the team logo, with the league's commissioner, my agent, attorneys, and the coaches, where we are met by camera flashes.

I swear, at this rate, I'll be blind by the time I'm thirty.

"We'd like to make a statement before we take any questions," the commissioner says, holding up his hands to quiet the crowd. "Our first order of business is to formally apologize to Isaiah Harrison."

He turns to me, and that's my cue to join him at the podium. As rehearsed, Sophie walks with me and stands just behind me and to my left.

"As a result of the extensive investigation that began as a result of accusations, it's been determined that Ike is completely innocent of all of the accusations made against him." He turns back to me. "I want to express how sorry I am that you had to go through such a rigorous investigation because of false allegations made against you. We are proud to have you in our league."

"Thank you." I shake his hand and then step to the microphone. "I'm not going to take any questions today, but I do want to make a statement. I want to thank everyone involved with the team, my coaches, and all of the third-party individuals who worked so tirelessly to prove to everyone that I was innocent. I love this game too much to ever do something to jeopardize my career. I also have too much respect for Seattle. This city has embraced me with nothing but kindness and support, and I just couldn't love it more."

I glance back at Sophie, who grins at me.

"And finally, I need to thank my girlfriend, Sophie

Montgomery, and her entire family for of their support through all of this. I didn't know that a family could be so encouraging, so accepting, and so unconditionally supportive until I met you and your family. I love you, baby."

I glance back again in time to see her say, "I love you, too."

I step away from the podium, ignoring the questions being hurled my way.

The press doesn't like to be told no.

"Before we go, we have another announcement," the commissioner says, quieting the crowd. "This information will be made public later today anyway, so we might as well comment on it now. Florence Paddington is now officially the *former* owner of this Seattle team. During the same investigation, it was found that she engaged in gambling and actively tried to sabotage her own team, which is a gross violation of the league's personal code of conduct. Therefore Florence was forced to sell immediately and is facing charges for a list of things that I cannot comment on at this time, as part of the investigation is still ongoing, and for legal reasons, this is all I can say."

The crowd explodes with questions, but we simply wave, thank everyone for coming, and walk off the small stage.

"I'm glad that's over," I mutter, and Coach Mac hears me.

"You and me both. Now, let's move on and focus on

the upcoming season."

"That's the best idea I've heard in a long time."

IT's MOVING DAY. It's been a month since the press conference. Since life got back to somewhat normal.

After that, I finally talked Sophie into moving in with me.

Not that I had to do much persuading.

Her condo sold in under a week, and today, we're moving her out.

"I have a question." I flag Soph over from where she's chatting with Olivia, who came to help us today, along with Vaughn and a multitude of other cousins whose names I'm still learning.

Buster's at the compound today, where I swear he's happier than at my house.

"What's up?" She skips over to me and pushes her hands into her back pockets, showing off those gorgeous tits.

"Do you want this couch in the house at Alki or in the beach house on the island?"

My lips twitch when she frowns in confusion.

"What house on the island?"

"The one I bought you."

"Whoa, he bought her a *house*," I hear someone say in a loud whisper.

"We have a house on the *island*?" she asks.

"Yes. Now, before you yell at me, I'm not signing the closing papers until you've seen it, so you can still veto it if you hate it, but it has the view you want and a huge backyard so we can invite your entire family over for parties."

She squeaks and then launches herself into my arms, hugging my neck so tight I might suffocate.

"Can't breathe."

"You bought us a *house.*"

"If you want it." She lets go of me, and I brush a strand of hair off her cheek. "Maybe we can even get married there. The backyard is big enough, I think."

Now, she just blinks at me. "What?"

"You think I'm *not* marrying you? Silly girl." I kiss her, set her on her feet, and then kneel before her, pulling the ring out of my pocket. "Sophie Montgomery, will you please put me out of my misery and marry me?"

"You're not miserable." But she grins and holds her hand out for the ring. "But yes. Yes, absolutely, Ike Harrison. I'll marry you."

I slide the ring onto her finger, and it fits perfectly. And then there are photos snapped, and we're wrapped in love and hearty congratulations.

For the first time in my life, I'm being pulled into a family that actually loves me for *me* and not for what I can do for them.

I have to get used to that.

But for Sophie, I'll do anything.

EPILOGUE

SOPHIE

Two Months Later

"*J*ke Harrison makes the touchdown!"

I jump out of my seat and scream and clap, even though I know he can't hear me. It's the first home game of the season, and he's killing it.

"That's the third one in two quarters," I say with excitement, and high-five Keaton, who's sitting next to me. "My fiancé is a badass."

"It's good that you're excited. Every camera is currently pointed up here to get your reaction."

"It's okay." I shrug and smile down at the field. "It's just the way it's going to be. I can deal. How about you?"

"No one cares that I'm here."

"No, silly. Speaking of being famous, how did things go with Sidney? You never did tell me."

"We had fun," is all he says.

"That's code for we had sex."

He just smirks.

"And then?"

"And then nothing."

I goggle at him. "Keaton Williams, you had a one-night stand with Sidney Sterling?"

"It's complicated."

"No, I don't think it is. In fact, I think it's just a yes or no question."

"Okay, I don't want to sit with you anymore."

Suddenly, there's a commotion on the field, and our team intercepts the ball, causing a turnover for the opposing team.

Keaton stays where he is as we watch Ike take the field once more. He calls the play, and when it's hiked back to him, there's no one open to pass to.

So, he runs it.

He dodges and swerves, making it into the end zone and giving Seattle yet *another* touchdown.

I'm losing my mind and watch as Ike turns his head up to me and points my way as he runs down the field.

I love you, too, babe.

BONUS EPILOGUE

ISAAC MONTGOMERY

One Year Later

"It was only twenty minutes ago that she was a tiny thing, all wrinkled and angry, screaming at the world as if she didn't just change my life forever."

Stacy takes my hand in hers and leans against me. We're standing in our daughter's backyard on the island across the Puget Sound from Seattle that she shares with her new husband, Ike.

And I'm all up in my feelings, as the kids say.

She's dancing with him, looking up into his face like he hung the moon.

She's looking at Ike the way she used to look at me when she was a little girl and *I* was her hero.

Today, I handed her over to another man. One who loves her more than anything but will never love her the way I can.

"She adores you," Stacy reminds me. "And that will never change."

I know that. My brain knows it. But my heart aches as Ike leads her over the dance floor that they had brought in just for this occasion.

Lights twinkle overhead, and there's still enough light left in the sky that we can see the ocean.

Everything, down to the last detail, is exactly as Sophie wanted it to be. I've heard everyone say how beautiful the flowers are, how good the food is, and how lovely the ceremony was.

But I only have eyes for my girl today.

When the song ends, I walk out to the floor and shake Ike's hand, then take Sophie into my arms as the band plays our song.

It's an old James Taylor song about going to Carolina, and it's one that I used to sing to Sophie at bedtime.

"I can't believe we pulled it off," Sophie says with a glowing smile. "It feels like it took *forever*."

"It was the blink of an eye," I reply simply. "And I'm not just talking about your engagement, either. You grew up so fast. There were times I felt like I couldn't keep up with you."

"Time flies when you're having fun. Thank you for today. You didn't have to pay for all of this, you know."

"Of course, I did. My daughter gets married. Her parents pay for it. But, I'm telling you right now, this one better stick because I'm not paying for another one."

Soph giggles and presses her cheek against mine. "I'm never doing this again, either, so it better stick. I love that Ike's mom came to spend a few weeks with us before the wedding so I could get to know her better. She's really sweet."

"I was shocked as hell that his dad showed up."

"We were, too," she murmurs. "Ike felt like he had to invite him, but we thought for sure he'd decline. But he didn't. He came in yesterday, and he says he's leaving tomorrow. He hasn't been bad to Melanie, either. Did you hear that their divorce is final? Melanie is living in Florida and loving it. And Clark had to go back to work, even though he sold the house Ike gave him."

"I think the work is good for him. It might help him stay out of trouble. I don't know, but maybe the anger has worn off, and now he's just ashamed," I murmur. "It was nice that you lit a candle for your friend, Steph."

"I feel like I owe her a lot," she says and looks up at me. "As tragic as it was to lose her, it's because of her that I do what I do and really have what I have. I hate that she's gone, and I won't forget her."

"No, you won't."

"Did you arrange for the sunset to happen while we're dancing?"

I smile over to where she's looking and see that the sky is bright orange and pink over the ocean.

"I don't know if I have that kind of pull."

"Are you kidding? You're my daddy. You can do literally *anything*."

"I'm glad you think so. You know, all jokes aside, if you ever need *anything*, all you have to do is call, and your mom and I will be right there."

"As always," she says with a smile. "I know, Dad. You've looked so sad all day today. You don't have to be."

"I'm not sad. I don't know what I am. I know that I'm happy for you and so proud of you. I like Ike, and I know he'll be a good husband. It's just hard to watch your daughter grow even further away from you."

"I'm never gonna be far."

The song ends, and she lifts up on her tiptoes to kiss my cheek. "I love you, Daddy."

"I love you, too, baby girl."

There's applause as we leave the floor, and then the band invites everyone else to dance the night away, and I pull my gorgeous wife into my arms.

"Isn't she pretty?" Stacy asks as she gazes at Sophie, who's now dancing with Liam. "We made gorgeous babies, Isaac Montgomery."

"She looks just like her mom, thank God."

"I think they're a nice mix of the two of us."

I look over to where my parents are swaying back and forth, still happily married and still so much in love.

And then my gaze wanders to the other couples.

Some around our age are empty nesters who are finding their way through what that entails.

And then to the young ones. Our kids. Some are paired off, married, and in love. Others still are just figuring out life.

"I'm grateful," I say out of the blue, surprising my wife. "God, Stace, I'm so fucking grateful for what we have. For you."

"The older we get, the more sentimental we become," she replies with a laugh. "But I guess that's okay. I'm grateful, too, babe. Look at everything you've given me."

"We built it together." I spin her around quickly, determined to shake off this melancholy and enjoy my wife. Enjoy this night. "Have I mentioned how smokin' hot you are in this dress?"

"No, actually."

"Well, I should be divorced for that alone."

"You've had a lot on your mind." She reaches up to brush her fingers through my hair, and just as it's always done, it sends shivers down my arms.

"I have a surprise for you."

She raises a brow, waiting.

"I'm taking *you* on a honeymoon since we never had one when we got married."

"Really? Where are we going?"

"Anywhere in the world you want."

"Oh, somewhere tropical. Maybe the Bahamas. But

no cruise. I don't want to float around on the ocean. That gives me the creeps."

I laugh and lean in to kiss her. "No cruise. Somewhere tropical works for me. That means you'll be mostly naked most of the time."

"Find the right location, and I can be all the way naked."

"As fun as that sounds, I'd have to kill someone for looking at you."

She giggles, and it sounds just like Sophie's earlier.

"I love you, Isaac."

"I love you more."

ABOUT THE AUTHOR

Kristen Proby has published more than sixty titles, many of which have hit the USA Today, New York Times and Wall Street Journal Bestsellers lists.

Kristen and her husband, John, make their home in her hometown of Whitefish, Montana with their two cats and dog.

facebook.com/booksbykristenproby

instagram.com/kristenproby

bookbub.com/profile/kristen-proby

goodreads.com/kristenproby

NEWSLETTER SIGN UP

I hope you enjoyed reading this story as much as I enjoyed writing it! For upcoming book news, be sure to join my newsletter! I promise I will only send you news-filled mail, and none of the spam. You can sign up here:

https://mailchi.mp/kristenproby.com/newsletter-sign-up

ALSO BY KRISTEN PROBY:

Other Books by Kristen Proby

The Single in Seattle Series
The Secret
The Surprise
The Scandal

The With Me In Seattle Series

Come Away With Me
Under The Mistletoe With Me
Fight With Me
Play With Me
Rock With Me
Safe With Me
Tied With Me

Breathe With Me

Forever With Me

Stay With Me

Indulge With Me

Love With Me

Dance With Me

Dream With Me

You Belong With Me

Imagine With Me

Shine With Me

Escape With Me

Flirt With Me

Change With Me

Take a Chance With Me

Check out the full series here: https://www.
kristenprobyauthor.com/with-me-in-seattle

The Big Sky Universe

Love Under the Big Sky

Loving Cara

Seducing Lauren

Falling for Jillian

Saving Grace

The Big Sky

Charming Hannah

Kissing Jenna
Waiting for Willa
Soaring With Fallon

Big Sky Royal
Enchanting Sebastian
Enticing Liam
Taunting Callum

Heroes of Big Sky
Honor
Courage
Shelter

Check out the full Big Sky universe here: https://
www.kristenprobyauthor.com/under-the-big-sky

Bayou Magic
Shadows
Spells
Serendipity

Check out the full series here: https://www.
kristenprobyauthor.com/bayou-magic

The Romancing Manhattan Series

All the Way

All it Takes

After All

Check out the full series here: https://www.
kristenprobyauthor.com/romancing-manhattan

The Boudreaux Series

Easy Love

Easy Charm

Easy Melody

Easy Kisses

Easy Magic

Easy Fortune

Easy Nights

Check out the full series here: https://www.
kristenprobyauthor.com/boudreaux

The Fusion Series

Listen to Me

Close to You

Blush for Me

The Beauty of Us

Savor You

Check out the full series here: https://www.
kristenprobyauthor.com/fusion

From 1001 Dark Nights

Easy With You

Easy For Keeps

No Reservations

Tempting Brooke

Wonder With Me

Shine With Me

Kristen Proby's Crossover Collection

Soaring with Fallon, A Big Sky Novel

Wicked Force: A Wicked Horse Vegas/Big Sky Novella
By Sawyer Bennett

All Stars Fall: A Seaside Pictures/Big Sky Novella
By Rachel Van Dyken

Hold On: A Play On/Big Sky Novella
By Samantha Young

Worth Fighting For: A Warrior Fight Club/Big Sky
Novella
By Laura Kaye

Crazy Imperfect Love: A Dirty Dicks/Big Sky Novella
By K.L. Grayson

Nothing Without You: A Forever Yours/Big Sky
Novella
By Monica Murphy

Check out the entire Crossover Collection here:
https://www.kristenprobyauthor.com/kristen-proby-
crossover-collection

Made in the USA
Las Vegas, NV
26 January 2023

66285047R00173